ACADEMIA

Academia

A. L. HOUSE

Academia

By A.L. House

Chapter 1

Angelina

I hate teaching. I like information, I like doing research, and I like presentations, but one thing having a parent in the public school system has taught me was "do not go into teaching" because no level of minuscule pay is worth the headache. Fortunately for me I had no intention of spending a career teaching students, unfortunately it was a requirement for my thesis funding. If I wanted to continue to eat I had to teach and do all the other responsibilities associated with that. That also included all the meetings like the one I was going to now. It was an introduction meeting to remind us all we were working for school, all the polices, and the material for the first week of classes, which was also useless for me. I had taught this class for the past year along with my two lab mates. I walked into the beginning of semester meeting with one of my lab mates, Shelia. Sheila was a master's student in the lab and she looked like most guys dream goth girl. Black hair, a body that spoke of going to the gym often, and dark blue eyes. The perfect dark to my blonde, light features. She also loved wearing rock band shirts from concerts of bands she had attended and I had never heard of unless it was in her car. Add in her midwestern manners and most people were goners before they realized her sarcasm was a deadly weapon. We decided to walk to the meeting together so we would have someone to complain to throughout the meeting.

"I swear this meeting just serves as a way to drag us all onto campus before we want to be here. I mean labs don't start for another week, why make us come back sooner?" Shelia complained as we walked towards the meeting room. They were hosting the meeting in some lab room that would inevitably barely fit all of us teaching the class.

"Because this school serves to torture us and not in the fun way." I say with a laugh.

"There's a fun way?"

Sheila and I turned to see our five-foot labmate, Rochel, who was also heading into the meeting. She was a latina with traditional features, a fiery personality, and a temper to match, but she was incredibly sweet to those she wanted to be friends with. We stopped so she could catch up with us before we started walking again. Rochel was an athlete and wicked creative but incredibly innocent and neither of us felt like explaining anything in the middle of our university hallway so I changed the subject fast.

"How's the fireman?" I asked Rochel. She was dating a professional firefighter and they had been together for about a year. He seemed nice, but I honestly didn't know much about him.

"He's good. He's picking me up after this." She said. Her short responses like this were why I didn't know much about him. Honestly, she never seemed to want to talk about him unless she had been drinking and even then it was minimal. We had mostly chalked it up to her being private about her love life. We walked into the room and headed straight for the back. It didn't matter how far I got into academia or how good of a student I was supposed to be, I was sitting with the other deadbeats in the back of the classroom. If I ever became a professor, I would be sitting in the back of the room during every staff or departmental meeting. The two of them sat on either side of me, ensuring the three of us could hide in the back for the entirety of the meeting.

"That's good." I absently replied while sitting down. I never knew what to say to her about him. She always just said he was good and even when I met him, he had as much personality as unseasoned pasta, but she seemed happy so that's all that mattered. I would like her to be actually excited about the person she was dating, but honestly I had zero room to critique. It was her relationship and unless I had reason I was not going to intervene. At least she had a love life, unlike me and Sheila.

I was interrupted from my musings by the head professor coming in roughly five minutes late with a "Happy everyone could make it!" Lateness is forever a pet peeve of mine, especially when I don't want to be there and the person who was late is annoyingly perky about it. Maybe I just dislike overly perky people?

"Let's get started for the semester! I hope you are all are as excited about teaching these students as I am. Once this computer comes up we will go over the schedule and finalize everyone's hours for the week." She proceeded to mess with the computer for another ten minutes while happily chatting away with Kendall the world's biggest brownnoser. The rest of us went back to messing around on our computers or staring off into space while contemplating all the actions that led to sitting in this godforsaken classroom. I would have talked to my lab mates, but I had the feeling Kendall would make a big deal about it if I did and I refused to give her another excuse to suck up and act like she was better than the rest of us.

The computer finally cooperated, and the projector flicked to life, showing the color-coded screen. The barely readable blocks of color highlighted each person's schedule, thankfully she had decided to put the names in the corner so we had a chance of finding our own rather than us just guessing based on unlabeled blocks of color. "Finally! The schedule is up on the board. Take a look and let me know if there are any conflicts."

I looked at the board and saw I had a class later today and a Thursday morning class, both highlighted in a disturbingly bright red. I did not want that Thursday one so I was hoping someone needed to switch.

"Can someone take my Thursday and I can trade for a Monday or Wednesday." said one of the guys from the back. Seems none of us wanted a Thursday class, which meant I was going to be stuck with mine. Typical, most grad classes were on Monday and Wednesday with the occasional event on Friday so there was never a reason to be on campus Thursdays. His class was taken by another girl and then the rest of the classes were stuck. Looks like I was keeping my schedule, hopefully, that class was pretty good and I could put my office hours right after it.

"Great! Now that the schedule is all worked out, let's talk about syllabus week!" She perkily went to the next slide, and I happily zoned in and out of the lecture. I had taught this class and others before so introducing material and handling the first week was incredibly simple. I was not worried at all about what I needed to have done but I had to stay in the room. I joined most of the others in playing on our computers while nodding periodically. When the lecture finally ended, I got up with Rochelle to leave when Kendal decided to bounce on over.

"Hey guys! How are you? Doing anything fun today?" She said perkily, while fully invading my space. In truth, she was a decently nice person, but kind of overbearing, annoyingly perky, and slightly condescending despite only being a first-year PhD. She also had a bad habit of sucking up to professors instead of making friends with other graduate students, which did not help her case at all.

"Well, considering it is a Monday during the semester. I won't be doing anything too much fun. Are you?" I shot back, slightly snarkily as was my defense against morning people, continuing to pack up and head up to my office so I can finish my coffee in peace.

"No, no time for fun here. I have so much work to do for this class and for my doctoral degree. Honestly, I don't know why I do it to myself, it is just so difficult. It truly is amazing to be able to contribute to science though. I am sure you all understand how hard it is for me." She said dramatically with a sign to seal how exhausted she was.

Considering I was in my third year of my PhD, I definitely understood but damn it is annoying for her to act like we were ending world hunger. Instead of engaging and giving her what she wanted I just said "Yep, I get it." and started for the door. Unfortunately for me, she followed.

"Well of course you do. Though laboratory experiments are so time-consuming for me. I don't know how we all find all the time to do it." She then started gearing up for a new topic when she was waylaid by a new TA who wanted to ask her about prior semesters teaching this class, poor unfortunate soul.

"Bye Kendal." I said while heading out the door. I saw Sheila and Rochelle standing safely away from the door with smirks on their faces.

"You guys are assholes for leaving me in there," I said while keeping on towards our office.

"And yet you love us anyway," Sheila said while following in behind me. Rochelle followed behind her. We headed up the stairs and to our shared office. The office had six desks, though only three of them were normally occupied. The desks were basic black topped with a large computer monitor on each. Four were against the front walls with the rest of the walls being bordered by black lab tables. Then two desks sat in the middle with the back one facing so the occupant could face the door. This was my desk. Sheila had the one to the right of the door and

Rochelle had the one to the left. The rest were for when the lab was bigger or if everyone actually bothered to come in at the same time, which was highly unlikely. I honestly do not think the lab was ever more occupied than the four of us in the room at the time.

"So how are we feeling about this semester?" I asked while setting my things down on my desk.

"It's going to fucking suck but at least teaching should still be easy," Sheila replied.

"I don't think it will be too bad, but I agree teaching is gonna be the easy part," Rochelle replied. We made some more small talk before slowly opening our computers and starting on what we needed to get done for the day. I had to agree with both of them, teaching was honestly easy in comparison to the classes we had to take, the research we had to get done, and the side projects that we all were working on. It was a pretty demanding schedule but also felt like we were doing nothing at all. It was an odd conundrum, but I think the flexibility in schedule and the fact that I genuinely enjoy the research, made it a lot easier for me.

I started listening to my music and working on the latest draft of a paper I was trying to publish. My advisor wanted this sent to the other authors by the end of the day, which might be tricky as two hours of that day were going to be taken up by teaching. My phone then pinged with a message from Ryan. Ryan was a guy I had matched with on a dating app about two weeks ago and we have been talking every single day since. He was cute and funny, but I was reserving judgment until our date this weekend. I had learned the hard way; some people were far better in text messages than they ever would be in person.

Ryan: Good morning gorgeous! Try not to drink too much coffee on the first day back

Me: Morning! The coffee is a requirement so define too much.

Ryan: I feel like if you had to ask that, then you might be nearing the too much area.

Me: Who? Me? Never?

Ryan: Uh huh, sure. Did you change your teaching schedule?

Me: Nope, still teaching today and Thursday, so I should be all good for Thursday evening!

Ryan: That's great! I'll leave you be so you can work on everything. Talk tonight?

Me: Thanks! Yea talk tonight.

Ryan: ◈

I put my phone face down with a smile on my face and looked up to see Sheila smiling at me. I just stuck my tongue out at her and went back to work. She and Rochelle had been wanting me to find a partner for a while, but I was so private about my personal life that I rarely told them about any serious dates. I just did not want to jinx it. Plus, no sense in getting their hopes up over a guy who was not going anywhere. After working for a few hours, I sent my draft over and headed out to treat myself to another coffee. I looked at my phone to check if I had a message from Ryan and smacked directly into a guy. Thankfully he caught me by the arm, or I would have further embarrassed myself by bouncing off him and onto the floor. My phone hit the floor beside our feet and I moved to grab it, bumping my forehead into his thigh. My face heated and I could not look up at the guy after straightening quickly.

"Sorry about that. Are you alright?" I said while staring at his black sneakers, my embarrassment still not under control.

"I had a cute girl's head on my thigh and got to hold her hand. In what world would I not be alright?" He said with a chuckle. His voice was deeper than I expected, and it startled me into looking up at him.

He was wearing blue jeans and a black band t-shirt. My eyes moved up his broad chest to a gorgeous face. His jawline was sharper than any I had seen, his eyes a crystal blue, which stood out from his slightly tanned skin and dark hair. I was staring for a long while until I was startled out of his eyes by another chuckle.

"Like what you see, sweetheart?"

I quickly looked down and my face heated again. His hand came under my chin and had me look at him again.

"Look at what you want, sweetheart, and hold that hand as long as you want." He said while squeezing the hand that still held mine from when he caught me.

I quickly dropped his hand and moved away. "Sorry about that. I am normally more together than this, but the coffee has not kicked in yet."

"Don't apologize. Unless it's for dropping my hand, cause I was enjoying that."

"Well, sorry for that then. I don't normally hold someone's hand until I know their name."

"My name is Rob. Can I have that hand back now?"

"Nope. I have to go on an important errand, but maybe another time." I said with a smile while moving around him and down the hallway.

"Hey, you never told me your name!" He shouted down the hallway. I just smiled and turned, waved at him, and turned back around with a new bounce in my step.

I was in such a good mood for the rest of the trip to get my coffee.

Chapter 2

R ob
The scent of her perfume lingered in my nose, and I could still feel her hand in mine. This girl really thought she was going to get away without me figuring out who she is? We literally crashed while she was coming out of her office and her picture is probably posted on the lab website. I was going to find my angel girl. Hopefully, it would be even easier than I thought to find her again.

Chapter 3

Angelina

I fully hate my office, computer, life choices, and pretty much everything that led to the moment of me sitting in a sixty-degree office and looking at the email criticizing the seventh draft of my proposal. I was supposed to defend my proposal in a few months, but it was looking like it would never actually happen at this rate. I looked at the clock and realized I also worked through lunch, so I had to work on my materials for teaching today and then go teach the class on an empty stomach. Fifteen minutes later I felt prepared for the introduction class since nothing had changed since last semester. It also was pretty basic first-day material so there shouldn't be any issues. I grabbed my stuff and the coffee that had been powering me throughout the entire day. I left the lab with Shelia and Rochelle still inside, who were so completely engrossed in their work that they hardly noticed me leaving. Thankfully my class was just down the stairs, so I arrived to unlock the room with plenty of time to set up the computer, pull out the sign-in sheet, and prop open the door.

The worst thing about the first week of classes is how awkward everyone is. Case in point the students who are too afraid to open the door to the classroom where their class is being held, despite the door being propped open for them. I refused to wave them in because this was something they needed to learn to do. If I waved them into the room now, then I would have to constantly tell them to come in and they would never walk into a classroom without permission. It might be mean, but it would make all of our lives easier. Also, it let me spot the go-getters, because they would walk into the room without a single care. After about five minutes the door finally opened with a girl popping her head into the room.

"Can we come in?" She asked.

"Yep. Whenever the door is propped you all are good to come into the room." I responded. "Please sign in on the sheet at the front and pick any seat at a lab table." The room was arranged with two long rows of lab tables in the middle. Fish tanks and tables lined all the walls, and a chalkboard, computer, and projector were at the very front by the door. This is where I was sitting on my stool while the students slowly trickled in and signed in on the paper. The first students chose seats as far away from each other as possible, but every seat except four were completely filled by the time class was supposed to start. I stood up to start presenting the PowerPoint when the door opened and admitted my final two students of the day, one of which was startlingly familiar.

Rob

Gotcha angel. I had looked up her lab online but without a name, I could not be sure which bio and information belonged to her. I had spent the rest of the time in classes thinking about orchestrating another meeting with her, only to have her fall into my lap as my teacher. I signed my name with a smiley face and winked at her as I went to take my seat. Unfortunately, she did not blush prettily like I wanted her to, but her glare was just as attractive.

As she stood up to begin the course introductions, I took the time to stare at her without her being able to do anything about it. She was gorgeous with incredible legs, a rounded figure, heavy breasts, a firm ass, and beautiful green eyes. Her blonde hair was up in a clip that I longed to pull from her hair and see how far it fell down her back. Her green eyes were partially blocked by her thin-framed black glasses, but her outfit did nothing to conceal her figure. It may have been a pair of blue jeans and a green V-neck shirt, but her figure was not contained at all. I was staring so hard that Jake kicked me under the table. I shot him a look to convey we would talk after, but I was not ashamed to be looking at the girl who would be mine.

Chapter 4

J ake
What the fuck is wrong with him?
I kicked him to get him to break his stare down of the poor teacher at the front of the room. Rob had not stopped staring at the incredibly attractive teacher for the last forty-five minutes of class. I get it, but damn the poor thing looked like she was getting uncomfortable under his prying stare. If he was trying to get her to notice him, I guess it worked, but damn blink once in a while.

Though now that I look at her, maybe we can both go for her.

Our group had shared women before, but never had we actively pursued one. Something about the blonde standing at the front of the room made me think she would be worth it. She was pretty, but so were a lot of women. What captured my attention was how she spoke. Yes, she was unnerved by Rob's creepy stare, I'd be concerned if she wasn't, but otherwise, she was confident and spoke in a way that captured all of our attention. That thought made me look around to be sure that no one else was paying her too much attention, but thankfully everyone else was mostly disinterested. The other students were either on computers, phones, or doodling on their notebooks with the occasional glance up at her when she turned a slide. They had no appreciation for her, which I greatly appreciated, even though she deserved all the attention in the world. I just wanted that attention to come from me.

I glanced up as the final slide came on screen.

"My office hours are on Thursdays from eight to ten in the morning, additionally if you need to make up a class with me that is the day you can do so. I teach on Thursday afternoons. Please email me before you decide to do this. If you cannot make that day then you can always make up the time with another TA on a different day. My email and contact information, including my office location, is on the slide. Any questions?" She said to wrap up her lecture.

Well, well, well. She certainly likes to make our job easy, doesn't she?

I thought about ways I could abuse the information she had so helpfully given us, while she answered inane questions from the other students. The majority of their questions were previously answered in her presentation or were things that did not matter yet, since they would not be an issue till the middle or end of the semester. Despite this, she answered every question with grace and put the students at ease.

"Any final questions?" She paused to see if anyone would answer her. "Great, then let's end early today and I will see you all next week. Good luck with the first week of classes!"

If I have my way, sweetheart, I will see you far sooner than that.

I waited along with Rob to give the other students a chance to clear out before standing and walking towards her.

"I am so sorry my friend and I came in so late to class; we got a little turned around. I promise it will not happen again." I said with a smile. Her green eyes were even more prominent up close.

She smiled back, before glancing over my shoulder and dropping the smile a little. "No worries, I understand for the first week. In the future be sure to be on time for class. I will see you both next week."

I stared directly into her eyes with a little smirk. "Don't worry, we won't miss a single second."

I then turned, grabbed Rob by his backpack and hauled him out of the room. Once we were in the hallway, I kept walking until we were outside of the building and unlikely to be seen by her. I then turned and looked at Rob.

"Alright I get it, I'm in, but he's also gonna want her."

A smile stretched across Rob's face. "I figured as much."

Chapter 5

Angelina

When did my students get so hot? When did this become an issue? Why did I even think this was an issue? It's not like anything could or would happen anyway. I needed to just get back to my office, destress from teaching and just forget all about the class until next week.

With a short nod, I headed back to my office I still had a lot to get done today and it felt like the day was already away from me. I still needed to finish my paper, send the draft, upload the slides to today's class page, and email my two students who missed and then I might be able to actually relax for a bit. I doubt it though since I needed to clean my apartment and cook dinner.

And somehow I think I have the time to actually date.

It took another three hours to polish the draft and I went to send emails to my two students who missed the class today, letting them know the first one did not count towards attendance, but to please let me know if they had dropped the class. In seconds, I had a reply from one of them.

Dear Angelina,

I apologize for missing class today. I was feeling a little under the weather. Please let me know how to make it up to you. I will be sure to be there next week and every week after that.

Marcus R.

I had to reread it a couple of times to be sure that I had read it correctly. Why did this guy sound vaguely like a Victorian romance novel? Maybe he was nervous, but the email was a little weird. I still had to reply to him, but I made sure to make it as professional as possible and just ignored the odd parts.

Marcus,

No need to make up the class, just let me know if you have any questions about the material. I will see you in class next week.

Angelina

My computer dinged again before I had a chance to even close the email tab.

I look forward to it.

Yeah, I had a feeling this guy was going to be a problem in class.

Chapter 6

R^ob *Is she seriously just now leaving the building? The IA meeting was at 8 am and she was here before that, it is now 7 pm. How is she going to eat? Dear lord, what is she going to eat?*

I watched Angelina as she bobbed her head to her music with her slightly bulging backpack strapped to her back. I did not understand how this schedule could be good for her. She did not even see the sunlight today! When she is mine I am definitely making sure she eats every day and has a reasonable schedule. There is no way I am letting her work like this all semester. She won't have any time for us if she works like this.

I followed her as she wove through the other students still milling around on campus this late, lost in thought about how I was going to get her to take better care of herself when I saw her head turn towards a brown-haired idiot.

"Ang! Hey! Sorry I missed you in the lab." said the flip-flop-wearing hippy. His brown hair fell into his eyes while he prevented my girl from going home.

"Jare! Hi! I can't believe I didn't see you. It felt like I was in the office all day." She replied while taking out an earphone.

That's cause you were there all day, sweetheart.

"Yeah weird. Are you going to the grad student social this Friday?" The dead hippy is now asking my girl out, wonderful. I also was going to have to figure out when this social was so I could make sure these idiots did not get too close to her there.

"Yep! I think all of us are! I'll see you there!" She replied. Now I was definitely going to have to figure out where this thing was gonna be.

"I'll let you get home then! See you Friday or in the lab tomorrow I guess." The hippy said with a laugh and then leaned in to hug her. How nice of him to sign his death warrant with a hug.

Angelina just waved at him, put her earphones back in, and then continued on her route. She never even noticed me following her on her twenty-minute walk back to her apartment building. I did not leave until I was sure she was inside and heard the lock click on her apartment door. Now I knew where my angel lived.

Chapter 7

Angelina

I never remember how exhausting the first day of the semester was until I had to follow the schedule again. I dropped my backpack on my kitchen table, pulled my meal prep out of the fridge, and threw it into the microwave. As the food heated up I unpacked my bookbag, fully knowing that the second I sat down to eat I was not going to want to get back up. I turned the AC down to a reasonable temperature, threw on some sweatpants, and my hair up in a clip just as the microwave made a wonderful dinging noise to tell me my food was ready. I settled on the couch to watch an episode of The Crown on Netflix, my guilty pleasure show, while digging into the food I made on Sunday to get me through this week. The chicken, broccoli, and rice might not sound exciting, but it tasted so good. Cooking was one of the things I loved to do, and it was what bonded me to Ryan in the first place. My phone chimed right as I was finishing devouring my food with a message from him.

Ryan: So, did you survive, or do I have to get revenge on a classroom full of kids?

I laughed before responding.

Me: I don't know; those kids might be hard for you to get revenge on.

Ryan: Well, how else am I supposed to spend Thursday evening if I'm not avenging my date?

Me: I guess you'll just have to spend it by getting dinner with me then.

Ryan: That sounds like a better option. I'll leave the revenge plans in the folder for now.

From there we talked about our days with him filling me in on his job as a tutor for a large online tutoring service. Apparently, some parents and university students started their appointments on the very first day of school. The little overachievers. I told him about the kids missing my class but left out the weird email or the hallway encounter. We had not even met in person and even though I was attracted to him, I did not think he needed to know every detail about my day, especially if it involved another man. I am completely loyal and transparent in a relationship, but the talking phase meant I had to hold back to keep from being hurt. I hate the talking phase.

Hours later when I was lying in bed and could barely keep my eyes open I sent

Me: Signing off here handsome, need to sleep. Talk to you in the morning.

Ryan: Sweet dreams, gorgeous girl.

Chapter 8

Ryan

"She needs to go to sleep sooner." I said out loud to no one in particular, ignoring the fact I contributed to her staying up. This girl had me wrapped up in knots when I had not even met her in person. I was not sure if she was real or looked like her photos. There may have been some light social media stalking but all that proved was that the girl existed, not that she was the one talking to me or wasn't using filters. Stupid privacy settings and stupid morals that didn't allow me to hack into her social media. She could have figured out who I was and was trying to catfish me for all I knew. I would find out on Thursday and if she was real, then she was going to be mine. There was no way I would ever let a girl this good go.

"How was class geniuses?" I asked my two roommates as they came in the door from the gym, barely glancing up from the millionth perusal of her dating profile. I could not wait till that was deleted and these other men were not thinking they had a chance with her. The roommates were later today than normal, but I chalked that up to them getting used to following a semester routine again.

The two of them looked at each other and then just smiled before heading to their respective rooms to take a shower, not answering my question.

Huh, weird.

I felt like I should interfere a little bit since they could get a little chaotic sometimes, but I was not in the mood to deal with it. I shrugged off their weirdness and headed upstairs to fall asleep to dreams of my online girl.

Chapter 9

Angelina

I always woke up before my alarm, whether it be ten minutes before or an hour before. I always woke up before it went off and was not able to go back to sleep once I did. This morning was no different. As I stared at the clock reading far too early in the morning, my mind woke up and began planning out my mental to-do list.

1. Emails
2. Meet with an undergrad student
3. Send in official office hours to the department office
4. Write conference abstract
5. Drink from coffee pot

Okay, that last one was not a to-do list thing but more of a requirement for surviving the day thing. I reluctantly got out of bed, switched off my phone alarm just as it started to go off, and headed for the bathroom to get ready for a new day. My bathroom light was only half working this morning which did not seem like a great omen to start the day off. I mentally added putting in a maintenance request to my ever-growing to-do list. Not that it would be fixed anytime soon. I started the coffee pot and then went to get dressed in the standard t-shirt and blue jeans that I wear whenever my schedule does not require me to look decently professional. My hair was thrown up in a clip and

I put on a pair of black slip-on bobs to complete the lazy student look. I was not tying a shoelace today. I grabbed a breakfast bar, poured my travel mug of coffee, hoisted my heavy backpack back onto my back, and stepped into the slightly cooler morning. One thing I missed about living up north was the nicer mornings and less back sweat.

The walk to campus was about twenty minutes with it being half uphill and half downhill. While this meant one way was not particularly difficult, it also meant that I had to trudge uphill ten minutes in the morning and then again in the evening when I was tired. The campus was surprisingly lively, partially owing to it being the first week of classes and partially to the students hurrying to their 8ams. By the third week about half of them will have stopped regularly attending classes so early and the campus will have cleared out some in the mornings. Unless it was midterms, or a bunch of classes had an in-person project that week.

I dragged myself up the stairs to my building and landed in my office seat with an exasperated groan.

"I am already over today," Sheila said from her seat. I evidently had missed her in my haste to get the heavy-ass backpack off my back and to get a chance to drink my coffee.

"Why what happened?" I asked while sitting in my fairly comfy rolling chair and beginning to set up my desk for work for the day.

"Check your email. He sent it to the entire lab." She said while leaning her chair back and propping her feet on her desk. Her arm went over her eyes, and she waved at me to hurry up and check it.

I turned on my computer with a sense of dread, realizing that it was likely my advisor had destroyed my day and made what I needed to get done for the day even less likely to actually happen. Sitting at the top of my school email inbox was the email Sheila had been talking about.

Lab,

We are meeting for lunch today at Jo's at noon. Be there or be square.

Stanley

"How the hell can he think this is okay? He just scheduled a lab meeting today with no warning, no schedule, nothing! What the hell! What if I already had something booked for that time?" I practically shouted. Thankfully the other grad students were the only ones in right now and we were all used to occasional shouting being heard down the halls.

"Not to mention unprofessional, but if we told him that he would lose his mind and tell all of us that we do not know what he is talking about or what professional means," Sheila responded, still in her laid-back position. I was beginning to think she was staying in that position until forced to move.

"So, we have to go. Anybody not able to?"

"I think Rochelle is not on campus today so I doubt she will come in and I think Constance is also gone, but I never know with her. The rest of us are definitely going to have to go though. He'll probably personally come and drag the two of us out of the office." She said.

Constance was one of the lab members that we rarely saw, with good reason. She had a full-time job and a partner with chronic health issues. The only problem is, she needed the support the lab environment gave her for her to actually make progress on her work. When she wasn't here for extended lengths of time, she did not make any progress at all, which only made the degree harder to get in the long run.

"Can we lock the door and pretend we aren't here?" I asked only half kidding.

"He would just smash it down like the Kool-Aid man." Sheila replied with a laugh.

"I guess we better get some things done then before he appears and drags us away to our doom." I laughed. Sheila groaned and reluctantly sat upright at her desk. Despite her response to our advisor, she truly did like her research project, but like any good night owl she just did not have any desire to do anything in the morning.

We worked in silence for the next few hours, the only noise being from the students in the hallway and the occasional noise from one of us to which the other would reply with a number score ranking from 1-10. The only noteworthy one was Sheila's 8.5 burp after she chugged her water to stop her hiccups that were losing a half point every time they happened. I was lost in my computer, my eyes aching and my legs incredibly unhappy with me once I finally stood up to use the bathroom. My standing broke the concentration Sheila had on her computer.

"What time is it?" She asked with a stretch.

I looked down at my phone clock, noting the myriad of notifications. "It's 11:30." I groaned. "We should probably head to Jo's soon. Let me go to the bathroom first." I walked out the door and down the hall, grateful for the opportunity to stretch my legs but dreading the walk down the hill to Jo's.

"We meet again Angel." I turned my head towards the voice to see Rob standing across the hall from the bathroom.

I kept walking and went into the bathroom. I did not have time for this today. When I went to the sink after, I saw the door open behind me and Rob crowded me against the sink, meeting my eyes in the mirror.

"You can't ignore me, Angel. I watch over things that are mine and I will get under your skin so far that you can never get me back out." He crowded even further against my back pressing my pelvis into the granite sink.

"If I'm an angel, how are you watching over me?" I said while staring directly into the mirror versions of his brown eyes.

Rob leaned in until his lips were against my neck "Because you may be an angel, but I will be your god." He leaned back and was undoubtedly taking stock of my heaving chest, flushed face, and maybe even the wetness leaking from my pussy at his words.

He leaned down and spoke his next words into my ear. "Don't clean up that mess in your panties, I want you to have a reminder of me for the rest of the day." Then he turned and walked back out of the door, leaving me to stare at myself in the bathroom mirror.

Fuck stupidly attractive idiotic men. What the hell am I going to do?

I went to the stall and cleaned up, splashing water on my face on the way out, before leaving the bathroom to a thankfully empty hallway. I went back to the lab and grabbed Shelia so we could head down to the lab meeting when my phone buzzed from a text message from Ryan.

Ryan: Hey gorgeous, what are you up to?

Me: At Jo's, I'll text you when I leave

I then switched my phone to silent, exchanged a look with Sheila, and headed to the table where the rest of our lab was sitting, minus Rochelle.

"Has anyone seen her today?" Dr. Stanley asked, not even bothering to clarify which woman he meant or say good afternoon to us as we approached.

The lab turned to me to answer like they always did. I always seemed to have the innate ability to know where the lab was going to be, likely cause I paid attention to them when they spoke and gave a flying fuck when they bothered to tell me things.

"She's not normally in town today, so I think she is working at her job since the school is not paying her." I said a little haughtily while staring directly at my annoying advisor.

"Well, that is no excuse for missing a lab meeting. I will have to speak with her." He said annoyed. The entire lab exchanged a look that said, "What do you expect when you don't give people any notice to show up to the meeting."

Sheila piped up. "Well, if she is at work, I doubt she has had the time to check her school email today. I am sure she would be here if she knew about it."

He snorted. "She was given plenty of notice."

I rolled my eyes behind my coffee cup.

In what world was four hours plenty of notice when you worked full time?

Thankfully he moved on to the lab updates starting with Kass on his left. Kass was a new addition to the lab. He recently arrived in the United States from Nepal and was incredibly shy around all of us, especially since we were all basically strangers to him.

"Classes began, nothing really to report yet. Just trying to figure everything out." Kass said.

"Well feel free to use us all as a resource as we truly enjoy helping everyone in this lab. I understand you are new but in future meetings be sure to have more of an update." Stanley said with a smug smile on his face.

Yea sure happy to do your job for you, yet again. No problem there, not like I have my own schedule.

The next person was Jare our postdoc. He did his master's and PhD in the lab and was a die-hard supporter of our advisor. He was a little hippish looking with long brown fluffy hair, constant large shorts, and flip flops no matter what the weather was like. We always were having to tell him to put his shoes on and he occasionally would walk across campus barefoot, having left his flip-flops under his desk in his office. The last time I covered his class, his students admitted he frequently taught without shoes, which is gross in those labs.

"Yea! The semester is off to a great start. Students seem energized. My project is off to an amazing start; I am working on writing up the proposal. My wife is pregnant, and my church is doing a potluck this weekend for any students or staff interested in getting food and meeting people." He finished with a smile.

Did he really just list his wife being pregnant with his first child in with the rest of his mundane updates for the week? Like he slid it in before the potluck? I locked eyes with Sheila, knowing she had the same thought.

"Jare is working on a project that is going to set him up for his research career and is doing very well for himself," Stanley said.

So we are all going to ignore the statement about the woman growing a human, got it.

I zoned out for the rest of the updates. Honestly, I likely knew more about what they were going to say than they were going to report to our advisor. The whole lab emailed and talked to me at least weekly about their projects, so I was well aware of where they all were. When it came to our advisor, less was more. I started looking around the place and seeing all of the people moving around, working on their own things, going on lunch dates, and felt eyes on the back of my head. Figuring it was someone else also taking a break and looking around I tuned back into my conversation in time to hear "Angelina, what is new with you?"

"Honestly, nothing major to report. Still sending drafts, which you have the newest one as of yesterday."

"Yes, I remember getting that. It will be a while before I can touch it since I am working on a proposal that is due this week."

He always has something due this week. I swear he either is the biggest procrastinator or the busiest human alive. My money is on procrastinator.

"No worries. I am also getting settled into classes and teaching. My two classes aren't meeting this week, so I just have teaching and research responsibilities. Everything is going well." I said with a forced smile.

"Good to hear. So that means you should be available to help out if anyone needs you this week." Stanley said.

I would've disputed it, if I actually thought that any of my fellow lab mates would try to add anything onto my plate. Instead, I just smiled and said, "Sure if the lab has questions I could help, my plate will be very full as of next week."

The eyes burning into the back of my head got even stronger. What the hell was this person's problem?

"Well, you all hear that! Be sure to utilize each other and..." I stopped listening as he droned on. Only tuning back in when he finally dismissed us. We all exchanged pleasantries and congratulated Jare on the upcoming baby. He then reminded us about the potluck again. Sheila and I made a hasty exit with a beeline for the taco place that was right next door for a quick lunch because, of course, he would take us to a place with food during lunch and not give anyone a chance to actually eat. I could have sworn on the way out that I caught a glimpse of Rob or Jake, but I could not be 100% sure.

"I'm going to grab us a table outside. Order me the same thing that you decide to eat." Sheila said as she headed off for a table. I joined the line to order while debating between the options. I felt body heat behind me as the person got uncomfortably close.

"Well teach, fancy meeting you here." I turned and saw Jake behind me so close that I could have kissed him.

I took a small step away that he quickly closed. "Good to see you again, just here grabbing food with a friend."

"And they left you all alone, lucky me."

Thankfully I was next and ordered four standard tacos, as I went to grab my wallet out of my back pocket Jake handed his card over with a "Add two more to that order. Thanks."

"You did not need to do that."

"I take care of things that are important to me. So, get used to being taken care of." He replied.

I was speechless as he guided me over to the waiting area. Thankfully the outdoor tables were out of sight so Sheila would not see me pressed up against this hunk of a man speechless over tacos.

He grinned down at me. "I like you speechless, I thought I would have to resort to something else to accomplish that."

At that, I scooted away from him. "Thank you so much. I will pay you back."

He heard our order being called, grabbed it, handed me all of the tacos, and said "Oh sweetheart, don't say things you really do not know the meaning of." With that he turned and walked out the door, leaving me no choice but to head outside to Sheila.

"What is with that look? Did your internet boyfriend send something spicy?" Sheila asked as I sat down with our tacos, noticing that we were getting three each. Thankfully Sheila did not say anything about the increased number. My stomach growled at the extra food.

"Nope just lost in thought. I have not checked my phone since we went into the meeting. I'll text him back after lunch." We set to devouring our tacos, Sheila then heading to the bathroom to clean up while I checked my messages, shocked to find so many.

Ryan: Who the hell is Jo?

Ryan: Sweetheart?

Ryan: Are you with another man?

Ryan: Text me when you see this

Me: Sorry. Jo's is a coffee shop near campus. Had a lab meeting. Just had lunch.

Ryan responded instantly

Ryan: You worried me. Thought I might have to fight some for you, not that I have an issue fighting for something that I want.

I laughed nervously at that message.

Oh boy, you have no idea how true that might end up being.

Chapter 10

J ake

   "She needs to eat more." I said to Rob.

"I know, when I was pressed up against her earlier I felt her stomach growl." Rob said with a smirk.

"When the hell were you pressed against her?" I asked, jealousy surging inside me, even though I did the exact same thing to her moments earlier.

Rob just smirked "In the bathroom earlier."

"And why the fuck were you in there?" I was seething.

"Isn't that where you go to get things wet?" Rob asked with a shit-eating grin. I hated that he had the idea first. It seems like Angel was about to have even less alone time if we had anything to do with it.

"If you scare her off, I'm going to fucking kill you."

"If she runs away from me scared, I'll help."

Chapter 11

Angelina

I still do not understand what is up with those guys, but I put them out of my mind in the interest of having a great day. Thankfully, the rest of the day mainly passed without incident. Well, I still spilled coffee on my shirt because I thought I was late for a meeting that wasn't till tomorrow. I also snorted so loud from a text that Ryan sent that Sheila nearly fell out of her chair after waking up from her mid-afternoon nap. She was teaching today, so that is how she chose to deal with the stress of her class. The one she would be having today was so bad that she had already gotten a warning email from the head teacher, which was mildly concerning. When overly positive people acknowledge something bad, the rest of us need to brace for hell.

Shelia left to teach around 5 p.m., and I decided that was a good time to check out and head home for the day. I had gotten the vast majority of my work done; I just needed to unwind and relax for a little bit. I was mentally exhausted, but I felt like I had enough energy to go for days.

Maybe a workout when I get home?

I used to hate working out, especially after my daily activities. Two years ago, I would have never considered it after a full workday and a twenty-minute walk, but I started to really enjoy Pilates and yoga in the last few months. They had a calming effect on my mind and also helped with flexibility. I had a feeling; I would need that calming effect to get through this semester.

Once home I changed into a sports bra and yoga pants. The main perk of at-home workouts was that no one was going to see me, and I did not have to drive to the gym. I queued up the video and started, letting my mind focus on nothing but the male instructor's voice and making sure my body was moving correctly.

Chapter 12

R ob
Why the fuck is there a man's voice inside her apartment?

I pulled out my phone and gave the guys a call. "We might have an issue. Come to Angel's, we might have to make a couple of things clear."

Chapter 13

Angelina

"Bend over and touch the ground. Be sure to really open your hips to feel the stretch in the legs and back."

I moved into the final stretching poses of the video, feeling good about the workout and my body could finally relax from the day's stress. I swear the tension of the day melted away as I finished my final roll up and the video ended with a namaste. Right as I started rolling up the mat there was a loud banging on the door.

"Texas police, open up."

What the actual fuck? Why are the cops here?

I answered the door sweaty and still in my sports bra.

The cop looked at me slightly embarrassed. "Ma'am I need you and any other occupants of the apartment to step outside."

"Can I put a shirt on first?" A little embarrassed at standing outside my house, sweaty and in my sweat-stained bra.

"I'm sorry ma'am, I cannot let you back inside the apartment. Please come outside." He gestured with his arm to a space a little away from my door, his hand nearly touching my arm to guide me.

I stepped outside and moved where he gestured. Of all the days to pick the worst pair of leggings.

"What is all this about?" I asked a little irritated as I now spotted my downstairs neighbor Ben, peering out his windows.

"There was a noise complaint made about a man and woman arguing at this address. We need to make sure both of you are okay." The cop looked at my outfit, sweat-covered body, and red face. His eyes lingered a moment on my red-flushed boobs. "Do we need to have a female officer talk about what you were doing?"

I blushed. "What, no! I am fine, there is no one else here. The only male voice in that apartment is my yoga video, which I had just finished when you knocked on my door."

"Ma'am I need to make sure that there is no one else here." The officer said.

"Fine, whatever. Then maybe you can go to where the complaint actually was." I opened the door and showed him around the place. I just wanted this over in case there was a couple out there seriously arguing, and the sweat started to cool on my body making me clammy. He even bent down and looked under the bed. After checking everywhere, he walked to the door and seemed to inspect the door handle.

"I apologize for the inconvenience ma'am. You have a nice night."

I fucking give up. Give me food and let me just go to fucking bed.

Chapter 14

R^{ob} "Well boys, no sign of anyone else having been in her place." John said. "I see why you were concerned though; she really is a looker."

"Keep those eyes somewhere else if you want to keep them." I snarled at him. I can't believe he walked her out of her apartment in that outfit, now everyone got to see what belonged to us.

"Don't worry about me; I'm not stupid to take on the three of you." John started walking away. "Also, her front door lock is shit. Professional advice is to get her a new one; her current one could be busted into with a credit card." He paused for a moment. "Not that I told you how to break into your girl's apartment."

John then got into his patrol car and left, leaving me staring at my girl's front door. Thankfully she could not see me sitting in my car from her door, but I had a clear view of the downstairs neighbor boy climbing the stairs to go knock on her door. She answered, thankfully with a shirt on or I would have to remind her who those perky breasts belonged to.

The boy dared to touch her arm and act like he was comforting her. Thankfully she did not let him into the house, or I would have to step in myself this time. After a few moments of this boy talking to her and trying to comfort her, he went back down to his apartment, stopping at the bottom of the stairs to look back up at her.

The fucker is in love with her, isn't he?

It seems I had another reason to add her living situation to my to-do list.

Chapter 15

Angelina

I woke up the next morning with zero desire to leave my house and thankfully I did not have to. Wednesdays were the one day I could work from home (barring any unexpected meetings) and I was looking forward to spending the day in sweatpants and a hoodie, despite the overwhelming heat outside I always stayed cold. I dragged myself out of bed, got dressed, and went to make myself a cup of coffee. I swear I would not be able to survive without the stuff and honestly, I had no interest in figuring out if that were true. The last few days had been incredibly draining and I really wanted to get some things done today while also being able to relax and recharge myself. Coffee finally in hand, I went to my desk to start getting some work done for the day. I needed to finish my work before my day tomorrow was taken by teaching and other responsibilities. It felt nearly impossible to stay on a schedule in grad school. A knock on the door jerked me out of my focus. A quick glance at my computer clock told me that it had been hours since I last looked up from my computer. The knock banged even louder.

Dear god I am coming, calm your tits.

I finally made it to the door only to immediately slam it shut. A foot in the door stopped it from completely closing and the banes of my existence barged their way into my apartment.

"Oh come on sweetheart, don't be like that. We left you alone all morning." Jake said with a cheeky grin. Rob followed him into my apartment with a similar smug look.

"What are you guys doing here? Get out." I crossed my arms and leaned against the wall. I was so irritated that they had broken my concentration even though it had been hours since I had gotten up. They didn't need to know that though.

"You need to take a break and we all need to eat lunch." Rob said. Right on cue, my stomach growled, betraying exactly how long it had been since I had eaten.

"What do you want love? Don't ask us to choose because I doubt what I want to eat will stop your stomach from growling." Jake said, nonchalantly leaning up against my closed apartment door.

"I don't really care what you want to eat for lunch, and I don't want to eat with you. Thanks for the reminder to take a break but I am not interested in whatever you are offering."

As soon as I finished Jake had me crowded against the wall with one hand on my throat and the other on my waistband. Staring directly into my eyes his hand slipped beneath my waistband and cupped me over my panties.

"I think you want what I am offering, you just won't admit it." Jake smirked. "Based on how you are soaking these panties, I think I am right." He rubbed his hand over me a few more times and I struggled to keep myself from mewling and rubbing myself against him like a cat in heat.

"How wet is our girl?" Rob asked from his stance off to the side of us.

Jake did not answer, he just pulled his hand out of my pants and held it out to Rob, without ever breaking eye contact with me. Rob sucked me off of Jakes's hand and I proceeded to drench my panties and feel my nipples tighten under my t-shirt. That was unexpectedly hot and I wanted to see it again. Jake took his hand back from Rob and returned to rubbing me over my panties.

"What do you want sweetheart? Do you want to finish before we eat?" He said in a way that made me sure I would be the meal in question.

"Come on now sweetheart. I am not giving you anymore unless you tell me what you want." He stopped his delicious hand movements and proceeded to leave me teetered on a knife's edge, a flick of his pinky all it would take to push me over.

"Do you want to come?" Rob asked. Crowding behind Jake and rubbing my nipples with each hand.

I couldn't think, I was surrounded, turned on, and just wanted to come. I nodded as much and as violently as the hand at my throat would allow.

"Good girl."

At that moment Jake pressed directly on my clit through my panties while Rob pinched my hard pointed nipples through my shirt. I went off like a rocket. I have never come so hard with my clothes on and the only thing keeping me up was their hands pinning me against the wall. As I came back into myself I slowly realized what I had done.

I came from my students' hands.

The second I began mentally spiraling, Jake kissed me so hard that I slammed the back of my head against the wall. I could not think about anything else, let alone think. As quick as it started, the guys backed away and headed for the door, leaving me gasping against the wall.

"Thanks for the taste love. I'll have food sent to your door. You better eat it all." Rob called over his shoulder as they walked out my front door.

The second the door closed behind them I moved to lock the door. My legs gave out on the couch as I started overthinking the encounter. That was until a pizza delivery guy interrupted my spiraling thoughts. The bastards had gotten me my favorite pizza and breadsticks too.

What the hell was I going to do?

Chapter 16

Angelina

The next morning, I woke ready to head to campus and avoid Jake and Rob. I had another class to teach today and right after I had a date with Ryan. Nobody was going to derail me today.

But didn't you love what they did? You have never come that hard in your life.

Stupid brain making stupid points. I absolutely did not have the time to deal with that crap today. I shook myself out of those thoughts and started getting ready for the day. I left with my headphones in, backpack on, and coffee I'm hand. All in all, it was looking like it would shape up to be a great day. I was feeling optimistic and....

"Morning sweetheart."

Optimism over. I turned and looked at the smug bastard known as Jake who was leaning up against my apartment building.

"What do you want?" I asked while continuing to walk away from him.

Suddenly a cup of coffee was placed under my nose, stopping me in my tracks.

"I want to bring you this and walk my girl to her office." He said, handing me my coffee and standing in front of me.

I grabbed the coffee from his hand and tried to step around him. "I think I can manage to find my way there."

"I wasn't asking." He said moving to the side and falling into step beside me. We did not talk the entire twenty-minute walk, but the entire time he stayed beside me, forcing me on the inside of the sidewalk, opening doors, and finally taking my coffee from me so I could open the door to my office. He handed the coffee back to me and kissed my forehead before I realized what was happening.

"Have a good day, sweetheart. Rob will be here later for lunch." He said, then turned and walked away, leaving me more confused than ever.

Thank God I am normally the first one in the office. I did not want to have to explain that one to Sheila.

I set the coffee down on the desk in front of my monitor and started setting up for the day. I unpacked my backpack and lunch which did not include any form of anything from the guys. I was not leaving this office until I had to. I glanced at the coffee I was given, seemed a waste to throw away perfectly good coffee, regardless of who gave it to me. Sitting at my computer I could not resist taking a sip from the heavenly smelling coffee.

Oh God, this tastes as good as it smells, how did he know?

I looked at the side of the cup to see what type of coffee he had gotten only to see "You'll have to trust me sweetheart." printed on the receipt taped to the cup. How the hell had he gotten a place to print that? I kept sipping the cup in anger when Sheila came in.

"Why the hell are there so many students on campus right now? Don't they know that the easiest week to skip is the first one? Go home." She said while chucking her backpack in her desk chair and letting the door slam close behind her.

"Bad day already?" I asked. Thankful for the excuse to put off the start of work.

"I got bumped into by so many people, and the bus was completely full. I almost want to hire some dude to drive me to the building, so I don't have to walk across this mess, or get an escort to make a bubble around me." She said while unpacking her back and putting her lunch away.

Should I tell her about my own morning escort? I mulled the thought while she continued ranting about the annoyance of other people existing. She spied my coffee cup that I was still holding and enjoying in spite.

"OOOOHHHHH that looks good! Where do you go for coffee this morning?" She said pointing at my cup.

"Oh, I um, grabbed this from the place down the street from me, was running a little early this morning." I stammered. There was no way I could say one of my stalker students brought his to me this morning.

"Nice! What did you end up getting? It does not smell like your normal coffee."

"I don't remember. I just asked the barista to make me whatever he recommended, and he did not print it on the side in case I hate it." I said while taking a sip of the delicious coffee. I was definitely never telling her the truth.

"I could never do that; I am way too picky." Sheila said, finally sitting in her seat and opening her computer. "Also have you seen the training seminar we now have to go to Friday morning?"

We talked about departmental things and what we had upcoming that day before settling into our daily routine. I had to work on a few things before I taught my class this afternoon. Hopefully, this class will not contain any frustrating students. Sheila left around noon to teach her class of the day and I took the opportunity to blare my music without having to have headphones in. Right as I was getting into a particularly raunchy song the office door opened and I quickly muted it.

"No please, I want to hear how those hips move at night." Rob said while closing the door gently behind him.

"What do you want? I am trying to work in here and my lab mates are going to be back any minute."

"It's lunchtime, so you need to take a break. And your lab mates are going to be gone until at least 1pm. So, you can eat with me."

"And what if someone comes in before then? You could get me in a lot of trouble."

"For eating?" Rob grinned wickedly. "Don't worry I will only be eating food today. You'll beg before I eat anything else. Besides if anyone asks, I am simply needing some individual time with my TA." He pulled a chair up beside my desk and sat down. He pulled out two sandwiches, two bags of chips, and a vanilla coke "Now let's eat."

I grabbed one of the sandwiches and he pushed the chips and coke to me. "Don't tell Jake this is what I fed you. He thinks it should be more healthy brain food, but I'd rather bribe you with what you like."

I opened the sandwich to discover a warm Italian sandwich made exactly how I liked it from a sandwich shop that was near my apartment. The vanilla coke was my favorite soda and the chips were barbeque flavored which was my preferred flavor. I just looked up at him in surprise.

Rob chuckled. "Eventually you'll have to come to terms with how much we want you and how much we know about you."

"But how the fuck did you know this?" I said shaking the sandwich.

"Just eat it love before I have to feed you by hand."

I took a bite of the sandwich in protest, resisting the urge to moan when the perfect explosion of flavor burst across my tongue. How was I supposed to mad at such an obvious violation of privacy when it let to something like this? Before I knew it the sandwich was gone and the bag of chips was opened and pushed towards me. I kept eating and watched Rob from over the bag of chips. It was surprising how the silence did not feel awkward. Instead, it felt like we had shared lunch before and this was just our daily routine. I kept glancing at him while I was eating, trying to piece together why this felt so normal.

"Did you want to ask me something?" He said with a smirk.

"Why?" I asked.

"Why you? Why lunch? or the why do we all exist?" Rob said, balling up his sandwich wrapping and tossing it into the trashcan beside the door from his seat.

"Why me? Why lunch? I'm not too sure about the last question?" I said finishing the last of my chips and looking down at the packet.

Rob grabbed my chin and forced me to look at him. "When a good thing happens to you love, don't question it, enjoy it." I sat there stunned at his words, not moving even when he leaned in to kiss me. What a kiss it was. I could not breathe, my body instinctively moving towards him, my hands tangling into his hair and pulling him closer. His tongue demanded entry into my mouth and it felt like he was eating me whole. When he finally released me I sucked in air and slumped back into my chair.

Rob chuckled and said, "That response does wonders for a man's ego." He leaned in and kissed my forehead before standing up and taking the trash. "I will let you get back to work now. Jake will be here after your class to walk you home. Thanks for a wonderful lunch and dessert." He smirked and walked out the office door leaving me in my chair stunned by the turn of events. The door closed behind him, and all I could do was relive the kiss in my head. Thankfully I managed to shake myself out of my reimagining with the help of my vanilla coke before Sheila had come back from teaching.

"How'd it go?" I asked thankful for the distraction from my mind's racing thoughts.

"Pretty good. It's hard for them to fuck up the first week." She said grabbing her lunch out of the fridge. "I still think we should not have classes over the lunch hour though, all they do is complain they are hungry. Then they complain when I tell them they cannot eat in a biology lab. If they knew half the gross stuff that had been on these tables, I doubt they would want to eat on them anyway."

I laughed because she was right, some of those kids would be horrified. However, they would find out later in the lab this semester so hopefully they would not be too horrified to actually participate in the class.

"Want to go eat lunch outside with me?" Sheila asked. "I noticed your lunchbox is still in here."

Damn it. I completely forgot that was in there still. "Thanks, but I already ate. I accidentally grabbed extra food this morning so that will be my lunch for tomorrow." I said hoping she bought the pitiful story. Eventually, I was going to have to tell her the truth about what was going on.

"Okay well, I am going to go eat and see the sun for once. Try not to work too hard." She said and then headed out the door.

I slumped back down in my seat and proceeded to attempt to get some work done for the next hour before teaching, to no avail. My mind kept racing back to Rob's words and that kiss. Just thinking about that kiss was turning me on and that was not productive at all.

I shook myself out of that train of thought and forced myself to focus on my work. All too soon I had to stop and head downstairs to set up for my lab. Thankfully I would be teaching the same stuff today that I had taught earlier in the week, but it did not mean that I was looking forward to it anymore this week. Thankfully the projector and computer were already on, so I did not have to wait for that. I placed the sign-in sheet on the table and as soon as I cracked the door the students already started coming in.

"Sign in on the sheet, so I can mark attendance and then find a seat. Today will be an easy day."

The students trickled to their seats and thankfully I recognized none of them. This class seemed to have their stuff together and the class went smoothly. Overall, I might like my Thursday section better, especially since it came without any overbearing men. When my last student had left the classroom it was around 5 pm and I knew I should start heading home to prepare for my date at 7 pm. I took the elevator back up to my office since the building was quiet and spotted one of my latest distractions by my office door.

"Ready for me to walk you home sweetheart?" Jake said from his position leaning against my office door.

"What makes you think I am ready to go home?" I asked.

Jake got in front of me, pressing his face up to mine. "It's 5 pm, you have been here for over eight hours, you are going home. Besides, you have plans tonight." He said moving back.

"I have a date tonight." I said.

"Yes, you do." He said, following me into my office and watching me as I packed up my stuff.

"And that does not bother you?" I asked, secretly hoping that it would.

"You already know who you belong to. I can handle a little competition until you figure that out."

"And what makes you think that I want to belong to you." I was getting annoyed now.

Jake moved and crowded me against the back workbench, my lower spine pressed into the edge while he surrounded me. "Your body wants it clearly; you are just letting your mind talk you out of it. I can wait a bit, but I will not wait forever for you to figure it out. You belong to us." He moved away from me and grabbed my fully packed backpack from my office chair. "Now let's go home." He said while walking out the door and forcing me to follow him and my backpack.

I followed him out the door and all the way home. Once again the silence was comfortable with him even as my mind was racing with his words. At my apartment I waited while he unlocked my door using my keys and ushered me inside. He set my backpack on my kitchen table, unpacked the travel mug and water bottle, and set my headphones to charge. Once finished Jake walked over to where I had been standing the entire time, grabbed the back of my neck and pulled me in for a brain-melting kiss.

"Have fun tonight, but remember who you actually belong to." He said. Then turned and left my apartment without giving me a chance to respond. My phone vibrated with a text

Ryan: Can't wait to see you tonight! I'll be the one in white!

I just melted against the wall. I was so fucking screwed.

Jake

"You aren't going to stop the date? Why not?" Rob asked as we saw Angelina leaving her apartment dressed in a gorgeous green dress that I just knew would make her already incredible eyes pop.

"Because this is the best way. Besides she'll figure everything out soon." I said still watching her as she climbed into the driver's seat of her car and set up the navigation on her phone.

"I still think this is going to backfire." Whined Rob again.

"Noted."

Angelina

We had agreed to meet at this swanky Italian restaurant for a first date. I normally preferred something chill like coffee, but he insisted that I not drink coffee after the sun had gone down. I drove and parked while also making sure my newest stalkers were nowhere around.

Forget them and just focus on the nice, normal guy that you are going on a date with. Not your psychotic students.

I went into the restaurant and spotted him immediately. Ryan was tall, blonde, and a large man. Not obese, just built. He was wearing a white shirt and black pants. He looked so gorgeous, and I started walking towards him. As soon as he spotted me, he stood up and walked towards me.

Imagine how well he would fit with the other two.

Where had that demon thought come from? Never mind, nope, nope not going to think about that.

I planned to focus solely on him, my date, and was ignoring all the other men that were trying to populate my brain.

"Sorry, hope you haven't been waiting long." I said when I reached him at the table.

He gave me a hug. God he smelled so good, just like a musky cologne mixed with the scent of man. I was intoxicated by it.

"No worries. I'm just glad to finally get to see you." He said. Dear lord his voice was deeper than I had considered.

He definitely would fit in with your other men. Nope, bad demon thought, bad.

He pulled out the chair for me and then went to sit down across from me. We were both silent as we studied the menu and gave the waiter our drink order.

"So how has your week been? I know you said it was busy with classes starting back up and your teaching responsibilities." He asked once the waiter had left.

"It actually hasn't been as bad as I thought. I like both of my classes, but I think my Thursday class is going to be more relaxed than Monday's." I replied, thinking about the two very annoying reasons that my Mondays were going to be eventful this semester.

"Oh yea, why is that?" He asked with one eyebrow going up.

As I went to answer I saw the two reasons come into the restaurant over his shoulder. They sat at the table directly behind him, somehow both managing to stare directly at me.

"Angelina, you okay?" He asked. I realized I had been staring at the two annoyances for longer than I had thought.

"Sorry, got distracted by an annoying gnat or two." Jake must've heard me because his mouth quirked up in a smirk.

"My Monday class seems to have a lot of big personalities, so it's going to be a challenge." I said, forcing myself to focus back on Ryan's brown eyes. They were pretty nice eyes to stare into.

"Well, some of enjoy a challenge." He replied, staring directly back into my eyes and making my cheeks flush at his words.

I broke eye contact and looked at the table, willing my cheeks to cool off. "So, what was your week like?" I quickly tried to change the subject.

"It's been good. Incredibly busy and I had to miss a couple of meetings, but I am hoping everything smooths out this week." He said.

"What is it exactly that you do again?"

"I own a company or two and now I am going back for my degree because some of the investors seem to have issues with the fact that I don't have one." He said, looking visibly annoyed for a split second before his face straightened back into a smile.

"Oh wow, that does seem like a lot. And kind of dumb that they want you to have credentials when they should just care about how well you are doing your job."

"Don't worry, I do my job very well doll." He said with a slight chuckle.

I blushed again, what is it with this man? Am I just making everything sound dirty for no reason? That moment thankfully the waiter came and dropped off our drinks and took our food order, saving me from further embarrassment. As I took a sip of my passionfruit cocktail I saw Rob over Ryan's shoulder suck his thumb into his mouth, his eyes staring directly into mine. I quickly looked away before I could get turned on by one man while on a date with a different man.

"Seems like you like your drink." Ryan said, gesturing to where I had paused with it to my lips.

"Sorry, I am not normally like this. I think I am just adjusting to my crazy schedule or something. Let's go back to focusing on you." I stammered and put my drink back on the table quickly. I had never been this awkward on a date before, though I had never had spectators watching my date before.

"I'll let you for now. Just know I prefer to focus on my partner until they are satisfied." He purred. "Now, tell me about the book that you were reading."

I proceeded to explain long-winded about my book, hobbies, and every other question he asked me. Every time I tried to turn the question around to him he either generally answered or deflected it back to me. It was almost like he just cared about what I wanted to say, regardless of his thoughts or opinions. Despite this, the conversation never lulled except when we were actively eating and I quickly forgot about the two men who were staring me down. When the time came for the bill, he never even let it touch the table, just handing his card to the waiter before I even had the chance to realize what had happened. Afterwards he stood, grabbed my hand and walked me out of the restaurant. Just outside of the door, he stopped turned towards me and asked "Which car is yours?"

I pointed to my crappy 2001 Ford Taurus and he walked me over to it.

"I had fun tonight." I said awkwardly at my card door. I always hated this part of dates.

"I did too and I want to see you again." He said, never letting go of my hand. "Can we do this, same time next week?"

"Absolutely."

"Also, I've been thinking of doing this since we matched."

He pulled me into him with the hand still holding mine and the other snaked behind my head to pull me into a deep kiss. His body pinned mine against my car and I could not help but keep pressing into him. I lost the ability to breathe, think, or do anything else but try to get closer to him. All too soon he pulled away from me and took about five steps back.

"Wow" I said, more in shock than anything.

"You can say that again." He said.

I unconsciously took a step closer to him and he put his arms up.

"Nope. Get in your car and go before I grab you again." He said pointing to my front door. I just looked at him.

"In. The. Car. Now. Or I will put you over the hood and have you making noises that only I should hear." He growled, still pointing to the door.

I blushed and went to turn towards my door when I was pushed against it face-first. His hand stopped my forehead from making contact with my door. His body trapping my hands against the door.

"Your blush, your body, just you. You do this to me and after getting that little taste I am an addict wanting my fix again." He said in my ear.

"Then take it." I said, bolder than I normally ever was, and arched back into him, this man was turning me on beyond belief.

"Oh, sweetheart I will. Just not here." He turned me around and pressed a kiss to my forehead. The heat of the moment still palpable between us. He then turned and walked away leaving me panting against my car door and my mind reeling the entire drive back.

"So how'd it go?" Jake crooned from his place beside my apartment door.

"Did you enjoy your kiss goodnight?" Rob said from the other side.

"Yes, I did! It was hot and wonderful, and you two can leave me alone!" I practically shouted as the two menaces followed me into my apartment. I apparently had decided just to accept the weirdness that was these two comfortably walking into my apartment all the time.

The guys exchanged a look and then crowded me against my kitchen cabinet.

"Could you all stop crowding me against things all the time? At some point, I'm gonna have a permanent bruise on my back." I huffed.

"Did he leave you worked up Angel?" Rob asked running his hands up and down my side.

"Do you need us to finish what he started?" Jake said, running his hand up the other. Their hands in the middle rested on my abdomen, both too high and too low to be of any use to me right now.

"I don't know what you are talking about." I said haughtily, trying to push them away before they realized just how right they were.

"So, if I checked your panties right now, I wouldn't find them wet at all?" Jake asked, his hand moving lower to the top of my pants.

"And your nipples are not trying to escape your shirt right now?" Rob asked, moving his hand higher to just under my breasts.

Jake leaned into me and whispered in my ear. "Tell us to leave or tell us to finish you. Otherwise, we are staying here all night."

I was tired, I was horny, and goddam these men were hot so I moaned out a broken "Please."

"Please what? Finish you or leave?"

"Finish me."

Immediately Rob pulled my top down and had one nipple covered by his mouth while the other he began pinching between his thumb and forefinger. Jake had his hand beneath my panties and began rubbing my clit using my embarrassingly wet self. I could not even stand and was only held up by their weight against the counter. I came within thirty seconds with lights exploding behind my eyes. As I came back into myself I saw the guys staring down at me, their hands still in the same places where I had left them.

"Ummm thanks for that. I really needed it." I said, kinda feeling awkward now that the haze of lust had lifted from me.

The guys just looked back at me and said "That one was for him, sweetheart. This one is for us."

They then resumed their activities on my now incredibly sensitive clit and breasts. Rob had moved his hand into my pants and was holding me up with two fingers while his thumb circled my clit. The tight space of my jeans not giving him much room to do anything more than flex his wrist to move inside me. Jake mercilessly attacked my incredibly sensitive nipples with his teeth causing me to cry out in a way that Rob quickly covered with his other hand. Their assault made me try to squirm away but their bodies trapped me fast against the counter.

"Come on Angel. You wanted us to finish you and we will, with one time for each of us." Rob said then turned his mouth to my neck while his fingers continued his work.

I came again in minutes. Their fingers and mouths not giving me a second to breathe. Rob's fingers had somehow worked their way into my mouth, causing me to have to cry out around them.

The boys paused and then Rob began pulling my pants down, his hand uncovering my mouth.

"What are you doing?" I asked, nearly too worn out to care, but I still tried to put my hands down to stop him before Jake grabbed them in one of his and pinned them to the counter behind me, causing my breasts to arch up easier into his mouth.

"I want to taste you for this last one." Rob said, lowering himself to his knees and positioning his mouth at my core. His intent completely obvious to me.

"Last one?" I asked kind of fearfully. There was no way they could expect me to cum again. I had barely recovered from the first one, let alone the second.

"We said one for each of us. The first was because of that dude. The second is for Jake, this one is for me." Rob said before beginning to lick at my panty covered mound.

"Oh fuck." I moaned brokenly. I was so sensitive that every touch from them felt like electricity stemming from my clit.

"That's it baby, let me in." Rob said, opening my legs more and shoving two fingers back into me. Jake continued his assault on my nipples, making them stand at attention while he sucked them into his mouth. Rob sucked on my clit at the exact moment Jake pinched both of my nipples and I went off like a rocket again. I soaked Rob's face and my legs shook so hard that Jake had to let go of my breasts to hold me up before I completely fell on top of Rob.

"Beautiful." Rob said from his position below me. He sat back on his knees with his face covered by my juices, two fingers still in my pussy, and I have never felt more powerful yet out of control at that moment. Rob came to his feet and finally pulled his hand out of me with a little whimper from me.

"I know baby, but I can't stay in you all day just yet." He sucked his fingers off and despite the three times I came I was horny again. "We will have to work up to that" He chuckled and grabbed me from Jake, finished stripping me and carried me to the shower.

"I am waiting out here because you aren't ready for us to take you right now, but you have five minutes before I am coming in after you." Rob said.

I showered quickly, leaning against the wall as the strength in my legs had not fully returned. Once I finished Rob greeted me with a towel and carried me to bed, depositing me naked onto the sheets. He went to put the towel back in the bathroom them came back to tuck me in. He then laid on top on the blanket on one side, Jake on the other, effectively trapping me between them under the covers.

"What the hell guys?"

"We are sleeping. Now unless you want us to join you under there, which will not be restful for any of us, I suggest you go to sleep." Jake said, rolling over and closing his eyes.

I decided not to protest and let their body warmth and soothing presence lull me to sleep in between them.

Chapter 17

Jake

I woke up in the morning due to the light piercing my eyes. I turned and saw the other two were still fast asleep. Angelina had her face tucked into Rob's shoulder and her hair covered the rest of her face before spilling onto the pillow, her arms still pinned under the blanket, but her bare breasts were outside the blanket. Her nipples pebbled in the morning air.

I longed to lean over and suck one into my mouth. Taste her first thing in the morning and have her wake up needy for us, but she wasn't there yet. First we needed her to wake up and be comfortable with us in her space. I glanced at Rob to see his artificially slow breathing, seems we both were up before our girl. I turned back over and waited till our Angel woke up.

Angelina

It's so hot, why is it so hot? Did the AC go out again? God, I need a new apartment.

I tried to move my arms to free myself from the inferno that had become my bed overnight, only to realize I was firmly pinned down in the blankets. My eyes shot open to see the shirtless men sleeping on either side of me, above the blankets, trapping me underneath. The memories of last night became crystal clear as I glanced down and saw my exposed boobs with no way for me to cover them up. I wiggled, trying to get an arm free without waking the guys up, and nearly had it when a chuckle from beside me stopped my movements.

I glanced over to see Rob laughing and then saw Jake laughing from the other side.

I glared at the both of them. "Were you just watching me struggle?"

"We were certainly watching something." Jake said with a wink and a glance towards my fully hard nipples.

"Will you two please help me." I said, trying not to stop my breasts from bouncing around while I moved.

"Sure I'll help you gorgeous." Rob leaned over and sucked one nipple into his mouth and I couldn't stop myself from moaning.

"We are here to help." Jake said before leaning over and sucking on the other side.

I moaned again and started to feel pressure building up in my pussy. I squirmed only to be pinned by Jake's massive leg, leaving me to grind on his thigh through the blankets.

Rob lifted off my nipple for a second to kiss me until I was gasping. "That's it gorgeous, take what you need." When his mouth returned to my nipple, my clit hit Jake's leg at the right spot and I came apart with a broken moan.

A few moments later I came back into myself with Jake brushing my hair gently away from my face and no longer being pinned by the blanket.

"How was that angel?" He asked, surprisingly tenderly.

"I feel good. It was different, but you guys have got to stop just making me come whenever you want." I said while working my way out from under the blanket. The second I was out Rob pinned me down, his brown hair falling into his face.

"Trust me love, we aren't doing it whenever we want, or you'd never stop coming unless we fucked you unconscious." He pecked my shocked face right on the lips. "And it felt different cause you had a nipple orgasm, we'll have to do that again cause you blacked out for a second." He said with a quick kiss to my breast before hopping off the bed and extending a hand to me.

"Now we need to get ready for school and you have things you need to do today." At his words I glanced at the clock and realized I was up well before my alarm, but I felt refreshed. I took his hand and let him lead me into the bathroom, leaving a pouting Jake on the bed.

Getting ready with the guys in my apartment felt surprisingly normal. Rob made another great cup of coffee. Turned out he didn't buy the first one he ever gave to me, but instead made it and packed it into a paper cup. Jake had my clothes ready and bookbag packed by the time I got out of the shower and dressed, assuring me there was a lunch in the bag. He also handed me my headphones and said they were fully charged. Somehow despite the extra people and distraction this morning, I still left at my usual time for my walk across campus. The guys also walked on either side of me the entire way to my office, each giving me a forehead kiss at my office door and promising to see me at my place that evening. I went into my office and slumped into my chair.

Did I just accidental myself into a three-person relationship?

"Date went that well or that badly?" Sheila said sitting at her desk. I was so lost in my own head that I never noticed her coming into the room or sitting down.

"Date?" I asked, before remembering the date with Ryan. Oh, fuck so much happened yesterday. "Oh yeah. The date went incredible! Really nice and I think we are going to see each other again."

She looked at me skeptically. "You don't sound too sure of that."

"I just didn't sleep much last night. Had too much coffee, too late."

She wiggled her eyebrows. "I was hoping that it was some guy keeping you up so late. Maybe the second date then."

Actually, it was two guys, and neither were the one I was on the date with.

I rolled my eyes and smiled at her. "Yeah maybe the second date."

At that moment I checked my phone to see the message Ryan sent me this morning

Ryan: Had a great date with you yesterday. Can't wait to see you again!

I closed my phone, and I quickly turned the conversation to departmental drama and the grad student hang-out that evening, while internally I was freaking out. What type of woman am I that I share my bed with two men after going on a date with the third? What type of woman also wants to have all three of them in her bed?

I shoved the thoughts out of my head and started working on some things before I met with my advisor at noon. I was determined not to dwell and let the day work itself out no matter what. The meeting with my advisor was standard stuff even though it gave me a headache from confusion. I went back to my office to hang out with Sheila for a little while before we both walked down to the local bar where the other graduate students were waiting for the grad social.

The bar was moderately busy, though it was only 4 pm so it was bound to pick up in the next couple of hours when the other people finally got off work. That was the issue with graduate students, we worked a lot and no one finished anything at the same time.

"Angelina, Sheila, over here."

We turned and headed to where the other grad students were waving us over. The customary pitcher of beer already waiting on the long picnic table.

"Hey guys!" I said while waving. The grad students were already in full swing and I'm guessing a couple of them had gotten here at 2 pm when the bar first opened, rather than waiting for 4 pm for the social to start. The bar Zolan's was a place where many a lab meeting, grad social, and other meetings were held for the biology department. Additionally, a lot of teaching assistants found it easier to grade at one of the outdoor tables with a beer in hand, at the end of the semester we had a final essay grading party here last year because of how atrocious the students' papers could be. I'm hoping we have another one this year because I doubted the essays would be any better.

Sheila and I sat at one end of the table across from Drew and Nick, who proceeded to pour us beer from the pitcher in front of him. Drew immediately dragged Sheila into a conversation about the stats class the two of them were taking and how hard it was going to be.

"How is your semester going so far?" Nick asked, setting the beer in front of me.

"Not too bad. I think my classes are going to be pretty easy to teach and I am not really taking any this semester so it should not be too bad." I replied, taking a sip of the slightly warm beer, the guys really had been here a while. "How's yours?"

"I swear the freshmen get worse every single year." Nick proceeded to go on a rant about his students that I mostly tuned out. He taught the same class I did, just a different section so I knew he really was exaggerating. The students could be a lot sometimes, but I doubted his were that much worse than any I had. I tuned him out and started looking around the bar at other people when a familiar back caught my attention. Is that Ryan? No, it couldn't be? Right?

"So do you ever get time off?" Nick asked.

I laughed, still trying to see if the back that was now sitting up straighter, actually belonged to Ryan. "You're pretty much looking at it?"

"So you'd be free next Friday at this time then?" Nick asked.

"What?" I said, now looking back at Nick. "I'm going to go to the bathroom. Be back in a second."

"I'll be sure to make sure no one spikes your drink." Nick said with a laugh. At that Sheila moved my beer closer to her and covered it with a coaster, never once breaking her conversation with Drew.

I stood and walked over to the bathroom, which was near where the Ryan look-alike had been, but in the brief moment I looked at Nick I had lost sight of him. I went into the bathroom and looked at myself in the mirror, thankful the two stalls were empty allowing me to take the second to recollect my thought. I had just started to turn to head back out when the bathroom door opened. I turned and Ryan was standing there, looking angry and staring me down in a way that made me remember the possessive force of his kiss.

"You know this is the ladies' room right." I said with a slight chuckle.

Ryan crossed the room in three steps, grabbed my arm and pulled me into the handicap stall. "You know you're mine right?"

"What?" I said, pushing against his chest. "We only had one date. You need to get out of here before someone notices."

"And apparently you need a reminder." He grabbed my wrists in one hand and put them behind my back before forcing me to my knees in the dirty bar bathroom. The other hand he used to open the fly on his jeans and pull out his rapidly hardening cock, despite the setting I licked my lips and really wanted it in my mouth.

"That's right sweetheart. I am going to fuck your face until you taste me and are reminded exactly who owns you." At that he shoved his dick into my mouth, hitting the back of my throat and making my eyes well up instantly. He started getting up a good rhythm and groaned when his dick went further down my throat. "Then when your throat is sore you will think twice before you talk to other men who want to see you on your knees." All I could do was gag around his cock, my nose pressing into his base. His hand had moved to the back of my head releasing my wrists and I started to move them down to reduce some of the ache building in my core. A violent pull on the back of my head, trapping me fully against him and his cock fully sheathed down my throat stopped me.

"Only good girls get to come. Not girls that decide to not know who they belong to." He pulled me off of him giving me a second to breathe before starting to fuck my face again.

"Or do you need to come over and over again until your body will never forget who it belongs to. Until you can't cry or scream or even move anymore. Until you are so overwhelmed with pleasure that you will beg but you will only get exactly what you need. Exactly the pleasure I allow you to have." At that mental imagine I groaned around his cock, causing an answering groan and stutter in Ryan's hips as he filled my mouth and throat. When he stopped cuming he pulled me off of him and pulled me to my feet kissing me deeply before I had a second to think about anything.

"Stop flirting with him." He said, with another kiss to my forehead before striding out the door. As the door opened I noticed two figures standing outside of it and I was worried they had heard everything going on inside. I refused to think about what had just happened and how much I had liked it. I looked at my mascara-streaked face and puffy lips in the mirror and started splashing cold water to clean up the best I could before heading back out to the table. A spot on the other side of Sheila across from a few of the girls was open, so I took it before Nick or anyone else could say anything. I was not going to chance Ryan a second time. As the party wound down, Nick came over to give me a hug and say he would reach out with times. I was going to have to figure out a way to let this man down easily before someone else broke the news to him. I then followed Sheila out and had her give me a ride home since I did not want to give my two stalkers a chance to suddenly appear. Hopefully, I could go to bed and chalk all of this up to a weird sexual dream. If I was lucky, that was what this entire semester had been.

Sheila dropped me off at my front door and pulled away. She was probably heading to the guy, that she though I didn't know abouts house. I wasn't going to confront her about him as long as she was happy. I shakily walked up to my door, the beer finally hitting now that I was essentially home and did not have to be tense. I pulled out my keys and headed towards my front door.

"I'll take that sweetheart." Jake said while taking my keys from my hand and unlocking my door. Rob appeared behind me and guided me into my apartment, a tenseness radiating off of both of them. Once inside Rob took my backpack and followed the familiar motions of unloading it and putting dirty dishes in the sink while Jake checked me over and asked me basic questions.

"I'm fine. I'm just tipsy now what the hell do you two want because I want to go to sleep!" I practically shouted.

That may have been the wrong thing to say because the two guys yanked me onto the couch with one on either side of me.

"We want you to take better care of yourself and to know better than to flirt with other men." Rob said, turning my face towards his to look me in the eyes.

Jake then turned me towards him and said "It seems that you need to be reminded of this, unfortunately, I refuse to fuck you while you have alcohol in your system."

I moved to get off the couch when Jake grabbed me and put me over his lap. "Let me go you assholes or I'll scream."

Rob started to pull down my pants ignoring the way I was wiggling on Jake's lap. They couldn't mean to, no.

"I'm thinking she needs at least ten to understand why she should not be drinking if we aren't there and why she shouldn't be flirting with men who want her." Jake said.

"I agree" said Rob caressing my ass. "I can't wait to see this ass turn a beautiful shade of pink."

"You are not going to" SMACK

My left ass cheek was on fire from the pain that erupted. I tried to move away from it but Jake's arm around my waist stopped me from moving.

"We aren't going to make you count this time sweetheart, but next time you are keeping count." Jake said spanking me again. The rest of the blows came in quick succession, five on each cheek and it felt like no space of my ass was untouched. Once it was over I felt hands rubbing my ass again as I cried.

"It's over sweetheart." Jake said. I then felt a finger going through my fold. "And I think you enjoyed it more than you want to admit." I arched towards the finger unconsciously and whimpered when he pulled it away, handed me over to Rob who carried me into the shower where he cleaned me off and applied lotion to my sore bottom. They then wrapped me in the bed the same way they did the previous night, only moving closer so that both of them were touching my bare skin in some way. Any attempts for me to speak were met with a kiss and we'll talk about it in the morning. I drifted off to sleep in between the two of them yet again. Surprisingly at peace with everything that had happened.

Chapter 18

Angelina

I woke up Saturday morning once again overheated and cocooned in between two bodies. This time though the hands were stroking my hair instead of trying to feel up my boobs, which were thankfully under covers this time.

"How are you feeling?" I rolled over to see Rob looking down at me from one side.

"Surprisingly good. I was expecting to feel more like shit because of how tipsy I was when Sheila dropped me off. " I shifted and felt the twinge in my ass. "Well aside from my butt which is a little sore this morning."

Jake ripped the covers off of me and flipped me onto my stomach. He started rubbing my ass in a way that was making me want to arch into his touch. "It looks good and pink to me."

Rob gave me a slight smack that had me arching away. Jake caught me and pinned me to the bed with one hand while the other continued rubbing his way around my body.

"Don't complain sweetheart, you still need to make yesterday up to us." Jake said, his hand moving closer to my core with every pass.

I tried to sit up again but was stopped by the hand on my back again. "Make what up to you?"

Jake's pinky had started rubbing my outer lips ever so softly on each pass. I was struggling to focus on his words and not grind into his hand.

"You flirted with that pompous guy." Rob's hand smacked my ass again, forcing a moan from me.

"You left your drink with him." Smack.

"And you got tipsy without one of us beside you to take care of you." Smack.

I got a little indignant at those words. "I am a grown woman and I can take care of myself."

I felt them both stop their movements, when I was then flipped onto my back so I was looking at both of their grinning faces.

"We are going to make you take that back."

"You can try." As soon as those words left my mouth, Jake slammed two fingers into my dripping pussy. Rob latched onto my left breast and pinned my arms above my head.

"Let's see. I think at least three for those infractions and another three at least to get you to take those words back. What do you say gorgeous?" Jake said with a grin and a twist of his wrist that made me see stars and come embarrassingly quickly. As I came back down his words registered with me.

"Six what?"

Jake pulled his fingers out and switched places with Rob who inserted two fingers into me and started rubbing my clit with his thumb. I was sensitive still and started trying to squirm away from his insistent hand even as the second orgasm started to build.

"Orgasms love." Jake said with a smile right as I began to come again.

Oh fuck.

Chapter 19

Jake

I could see the second she realized what she was in for today, especially as Rob started going down on her. The positively sinful noises coming from her mouth and his on her were making me so hard, even though we agreed not to fuck her today. Today was about reminding her who she belonged to and making her so addicted to us that she couldn't do anything but crave us. Hopefully, before she realized what we were up to. Angel came again with a broken cry and Rob's evil self kept sucking directly on her clit until she whimpered so loud I thought she would start crying. God, she was so beautiful like this.

Chapter 20

R^{ob} I pulled my mouth off of her when she started to shake again. I switched with Jake so he could go down on her and grabbed her wrists which were now limply laying against the bed. She had no energy left to even attempt to struggle. I started lightly sucking on her nipple while Jake started feasting on her dripping slit. I loved the noises she was making as she finally started breaking down. After her next three orgasms, she would fully be ours. She certainly would not forget what would happen if she did something stupid again.

Her head started thrashing again as her body built up to another orgasm. "I can't, please, I can't." She cried brokenly.

"You can and you will at least three more times." I said into her ear. "After this one, we will give you a little break, but you are going to come six times and apologize to us before we let you out of this bed. Now let go."

She came with the most beautiful, broken moan. Her body bowing upward before collapsing back to the bed, her chest heaving and flinching away from me when I lightly blew on her still pointed nipple. I glanced at Jake who was still sitting between her legs with a slick covered face.

"Good girl, roll over." I said, gently turning her onto her stomach so we could give her ass more attention while her pussy recovered for a moment. She weakly protested but still let me roll her over.

"Now let's finish what we started last night." Jake said before bringing his hand on her ass cheek. Despite how exhausted she must have been, Angel still tried to wiggle away from us but was stopped by my hands going under her body to grab her nipples and Jake grabbing her wrists in one hand at the base of her spine, forcing her back into place, now with her back bowed.

"What the hell?" Angel cried, trying to move from where my hands were torturing her sensitive nipples.

"You need the other half of your spanking." Jake said smacking her ass again. "Don't worry you don't have to count this time either since it's the same one." Angel stopped struggling and just moaned with her head thrown back and her tits arching into my hands while her ass pushed back into Jake's hand.

"That's our girl." Jake said as he finished the last smack. "Now come exactly like this."

Angelina stiffened. "What? I can't!"

Jake smacked her ass again, then shoved his fingers in before playing her body like a fiddle. I tugged her nipples and forced her chest out as her body quickly began building to another orgasm.

"You can and you will." I said.

She came with a cry that I could not help but lean in and swallow down. Her salty tears streaking into my mouth as I kissed her until she gasped for air.

"One more princess." I said while moving to change places with Jake. She simply moaned in answer, especially when I placed my jean-clad leg in between hers. I wanted her to soak my pants and work for this last orgasm.

"Ride my thigh love."

Jake sat her up on my thigh and I grabbed her hips while he got behind her back and twisted her tortured nipples yet again. She moaned and started grinding on my leg, quickly losing rhythm as I forced her back and forth. I had to bite back down a moan as I imagined her riding my cock exactly like this. Jake behind her, helping her. A glance at him, over her shoulder showed me he was having similar thoughts. Suddenly she threw her head back again and cried out before slumping forward into me. I gently laid her back on the bed and cuddled on one side while Jake moved to the other. We stroked her hair and side, avoiding anywhere that was overly sensitive. She curled into me and reached behind for Jake before drifting into sleep, exhausted from the morning's activities.

Angelina

Once again I woke up between the two guys, on top of the covers though. This time most of my body was delightfully sore and they were touching any part of my body they could possibly reach.

"How are you feeling?" Rob asked me. He seemed to be the more nurturing of the two.

"Feel like giving us that apology you owe us?" Jake asked rather roughly for so early in the morning.

"What apology?" I asked.

"The one for how you put yourself in danger and said you didn't need us to take care of you." Jake said. "Or do you need another demonstration." His hand band inching down my body towards my core. I reached out and stopped him before he got any further. I looked at his face and behind the teasing I could see a little bit of hurt and truth behind his words. They truly wanted me to need them.

"I'm sorry that I worried you both, but I can't rely on you yet." I said, trying to be truthful, while remembering it had been a week with these two and I still wasn't sure what this all was.

"We aren't asking you to yet, but you need to let us take care of you when we try. Deal?" Rob said.

"And no more stupid bar decisions or other men." Jake said.

"I am still going to bars with friends and you can't get rid of all men from my life. I will try to let you in more though." I said. "Now I need to shower and eat before I get hangry. Or were you two never letting me out of the bed?"

"Why did you want another greedy girl?" Jake started drifting his hand lower down my body again. My body twinged and wanted to arch into the hand despite the raw feeling in my vagina.

"Get up and shower you two. I'll have food ready when you get out." Rob said rolling out of the bed and heading to the kitchen.

Jake pouted before rolling out of bed and then grabbing me to carry me into the shower. We quickly rinsed off with minimal groping before turning off the water, drying off, and getting dressed in my comfy clothes. Jake stopped all efforts when I attempted to grab a bra or panties, so my sensitive parts were rubbing against the rough fabric. The smell coming from the kitchen was heavenly as Jake forced me to sit on the couch before handing me a glass of water and telling me to drink. His hands never stopped touching me the entire time.

Rob came over with a bowl of some pasta dish and said "Eat." Before returning with one for himself and Jake. He then put on a comedy show before sitting next to me so our thighs touched. The three of us ate in silence, watching the show. Once we finished Rob put the dishes in the sink before returning to the couch and practically shoved me down on Jake before laying on me and throwing a blanket over us all.

"Are you two okay?" I asked.

"Don't question how we take care of you." Jake said, seemly comfortable from his place on the bottom. I settled in and went back to watching the show, the guys providing a comforting warmth. The rest of the day passed in a similar fashion with minimal effort on my part. Rob constantly bringing food any time I merely thought about a snack or wanting something. Jake kept rubbing my back, sides, and anywhere else he could reach. The two of them seemed settled by me letting them take care of me and by remaining in constant contact. I felt like a human stress ball the way they needed to keep a hand on me at all times and seemed content doing so. The only downside is that they must have hidden my laptop away somewhere because I did not see it once all day. They also did not touch me sexually at all the rest of the day, thankfully giving my nerves and sensitive parts a much needed break. The conversation stayed light, mostly focused on the shows or other observations, the boys never mentioning what we had spent the day before doing. As the day wound down we started getting ready for bed, the guys showing no signs of leaving. Rob materialized my backpack and began packing everything for something they had planned for the next day. My laptop is still not in sight, I'm convinced they removed it from the apartment somehow without me noticing. That evening we went to bed much the same way we had woken up, except all of us under the covers and entangled. It was concerning how comforting I was finding them in such as short space of time. I fell asleep hoping that I would not get my heart broken in another short period.

Chapter 21

R^{ob} I woke up wrapped around Angelina and partially inter-twined with Jake. I carefully extracted myself from the two and gently turned Angelina into Jake's chest, where she snuggled further into him. I stopped and stared at the girl who had so clearly stolen my heart wrapped around one of my best friends. The majority of my world was lying in a bed that I did not want to get out of, but we needed to go do something out of the house today before we became hard-core recluses.

I walked out of the bedroom and went to the bathroom to freshen up. I used the bathroom, washed my face, and brushed my teeth with my wooden toothbrush that sat on the counter in the holder with two others. I stared at myself in the mirror and the tenderness on my scalp and side reminded me of Angelina. Her hands sinking into my hair and pulling hard without even realizing it when her wrists escaped our hold. The pain in my side from her elbows and knees digging into the soft tissue dur-ing the movie. The marks she left on me, the same as the marks I left on her. I may not be as outwardly possessive as Jake, but I still had a desperate desire to claim our gorgeous girl. Shaking myself out of that delightfully sinful train of thought, I walked out to the kitchen to make us sandwiches for our trip today. Hopefully Jake would wake our girl soon because I did not feel like being the bad guy when he was lying beside her on the bed, wide awake.

Chapter 22

Angelina

I woke up in bed to a gentle hand stroking my hair and my legs entangled with a warm body.

"Wake up gorgeous. The mean man is making us go outside today instead of having a delightfully fun time in bed again today." Jake said against my hair while pulling me further into his arms.

"Hey!" Rob shouted from the kitchen.

I chuckled at the two guys' antics and then groaned as Rob came in and grabbed me out of the bed.

"Hey! Give her back." Jake pouted from the bed.

Rob laughed and deposited me in the bathroom with a kiss before going back into the bedroom. A loud thud and shout from Jake meant that Rob had most likely tipped him out of the bed. I laughed from the bathroom which resulted in Jake running in to tickle me before being dragged out by Rob. I did my morning bathroom routine and headed into the bedroom to find one of the few athletic sets I owned sitting on the bed.

"Does somebody want to tell me where the hell we're going?" I asked sticking my head out of the bedroom.

"Don't worry about it and just get dressed!" Rob replied from the kitchen. Jake laughed from his place in the bathroom.

I got dressed in the matching black set and put on the socks that were laid out for me. The guys had even thought to lay out comfortable underwear and sports bra for a hopefully minimally athletic activity. I walked out into the kitchen where Rob was shoving more food and water bottles into one of my backpacks.

"You do know that I am very much an academic and not athletic at all right?" I asked Rob a little worried by the athletic gear he was wearing and the fact that it was 8 am on a Sunday.

"Don't worry I promise you will enjoy today." Rob said with a smile that shot heat straight to my core with the memory of everything that happened yesterday.

"Not like that sweetheart. Keep it in your pants." Jake said with a quick kiss to the top of my head. Rob grabbed the backpack and we headed out to a black Ford truck parked beside my car. Jake opened the passenger door for me and closed the door behind me after I was settled in the seat. Rob climbed in the driver's seat and waited for me to be buckled in before he put the truck in reverse. I glanced in the backseat to see Jake glancing out of the window, his knees nearly hitting the seat behind me.

"You could have sat in the front."

A glare from both of the guys at that made me drop that train of thought.

"So, are you going to finally tell me where we are going?" I asked, a little concerned about what their plans for me were.

"We are going on a little hike to show you this covered cave we found a little while back. Trust me you will like it and we can enjoy the beautiful weather before it gets unbearably hot this afternoon." Rob said, his hand moving from the gear stick to rest on my thigh.

"And if you hate it then you can blame Rob!" Jake said from the back. Rob took his hand off my thigh to attempt to hit Jake before turning on the radio and putting his hand back on my thigh with a squeeze. Before long we turned onto a gravel road for half a mile before pulling into a dirt parking lot that had one other car. The guys hopped out, with Jake opening my door again, and they guided me to the trailhead between them.

Rob started walking down the trail ahead with Jake grabbing my hand. We walked in a peaceful silence for about thirty minutes before we reached an intersection. Rob expertly turned down the trail marked INFERNO seemingly knowing exactly where he was going.

Jake leaned in to whisper in my ear. "He comes here a lot when he needs to think. Rob probably knows these trails better than anyone else in the town." I smiled, touched by his desire to share something so personal with me. We walked along the sunlit nature trail for a while, just enjoying the comfortable peaceful silence of the morning and each other's company. The birds broke the silence with their chirping every so often and the butterflies flitted in front of us along the trail. As the trail we were on ended, Rob turned onto a trail labeled PARADISO and walked about fifteen minutes before turning onto an unlabeled dirt trail.

The trail quickly opened into a beautiful meadow filled with flowers and grasses. Sunlight streamed in from the break in the trees, reminding us of the heat of the summer day. The pine trees ringed the meadow as the trail meandered through and the butterflies flitted from flower to flower. It was truly gorgeous as we followed the trail around the meadow. The trail started curving upwards until we reached the mouth of a shallow cave.

Rob turned and started spreading a blanket at the opening. "This is where I always love coming during difficult days or when I just need some alone time. Other hikers rarely come up this trail since it is unmarked and typically not maintained, or they stop at the meadow down there." He gestured down and I saw a clear view of the meadow through the trees.

"This is beautiful. Thank you for showing this to me. " I was amazed by all of this and could not believe he was showing this spot to me. Jake tugged me down to where he was sitting on the blanket, and I loved every second of being curled in his arms.

Rob pulled my legs into his lap and the three of us sat in silence, occasionally commented on the day but mostly enjoying our presence.

I started drifting off on Jake's shoulder when he gently shook me and said "Angel my ass is numb, so we need to head back. Plus, Rob might eat us if we don't get him lunch soon."

Rob looked at me with a different type of hunger in his eyes "I'll eat something, that's for sure."

I gulped suddenly turned on, but Rob shook himself out of it and grabbed my hand, heading back down the trail and leaving Jake to clean up the blanket and follow us back. We made it back to the car much faster than we traveled there, with Rob never once letting go of my hand except to open my car door and gesture me into the passenger seat.

"Where are we heading to now?" I asked, having given in to the plans the guys had for the day rather than fighting them on anything.

"We are going to get some lunch and since I am starving, we are going to Kobe." Jake said from his spot in the back.

"Fine." Rob groaned, putting the car in reverse and pulling out of the lot. I had no idea what this place was, but I was trusting them again today. I turned on Rob's radio looking for any sign that he didn't want me touching his radio, but he seemed content with letting me pick the music. I started blaring a 90s rock station and relaxing into the music as we drove. The guys nodding and getting into the beat for the fifteen-minute drive to the restaurant. When we pulled in, once again I was not allowed to open my own door.

The guys guided me into the restaurant that was beautiful for a college town place. It had beautiful wooden tables, a large bar area to the left and booths and tables for all party sizes to the right. There was a black carpet covering the floor and the staff all had on black pants and white shirts that fit the overall mood and decor of the restaurant. The host greeted Rob warmly and immediately sat us at a table in the back right corner, mostly hidden from view of the larger restaurant. I scooted into the booth and Jake shoved in beside me, Rob moved to sit across from us, glaring at Jake. I shot Rob a curious glance.

"I wanted to sit beside you." Rob said with a bit of a pout.

"You've been sitting beside her in the car all day. I get her now." Jake replied placing his hand on my thigh as the waiter returned with waters.

I glanced down at the menu and saw it was an all you can eat sushi place. I loved sushi! I picked out my appetizer, roll, and sashimi on the menu and watched as the guys made their own decisions right as the waiter returned for our orders. They seemed to know exactly what they wanted and once we had all ordered I shot Rob another look.

"What? Do you not like sushi?" He said panicked.

"Wait! I thought it was your favorite! Was I wrong?" Jake turned to Rob. "Were you wrong?"

I laughed at the ridiculousness of these two. "Neither of you were wrong about that. I love sushi! It's more how familiar you two seem with this place, much less to request a booth no one can really see us at."

Rob looked at me. "We come here all the time with our other roommate, so we know it really well and the staff know us because of that. And we got a booth in the corner because as much as we like going and being with you in public, we know you might not be ready for that."

"We want you to be comfortable and have fun with us today. No stress. So, relax and trust we know what we are doing." Jake continued.

I laughed, giving into the moment and the fun. Our food came and we gorged ourselves on sushi rolls, sashimi, and pork potstickers.

"You are going to have to roll me out of here." I said dramatically when I finished the last bite of my California roll.

Jake leaned over and poked my stomach, causing me to groan. "I think we might have to."

Rob flexed his arm. "I'll just carry her."

The waitress came over with the bill and before I could say anything, Jake put his hand, so it was cupping my mound shocking me into silence while Rob handed his card over to the waitress. He removed his hand when she left and resumed his conversation with Rob like nothing had happened. I realized that was the only sexual move the two had made on me today. Did they not want me anymore? Was today some long, extended form of a breakup or goodbye tour? I stayed silent as we finished our meal, thinking everything over from today and yesterday. I walked between the two of them back to the car and immediately turned on the radio to avoid conversation. Back at my place I followed them into my apartment and started taking my shoes off.

"What the fuck happened?" Jake growled.

I continued untying my shoes, still lost in my own thoughts. Jake grabbed my chin and forced my head up to look at him.

"What is going through that pretty little head of yours?"

I started to shake my head when Rob grabbed my ponytail forcing my movements to stop. My head was effectively pinned between their hands, making me unable to move away from their prying gaze.

"Why do you not want to touch me?" I finally said with a small tear leaking from my eye.

Jake jerked back in surprise.

"Why do you think we don't want to touch you? We are literally touching you right now!" Jake half shouted.

My cheeks flushed red in embarrassment. "Not like that." I said quietly.

Rob chuckled slightly, his hold on my hair changing to one that caused my body to react to it. "She wants to know why we didn't try anything with her today."

"Cause we wanted you to know we didn't only want you for that purpose. We want you for other things too." Jake responded.

I suddenly felt embarrassed, realizing they also wanted to spend time with me, when I was thinking about them like a piece of meat.

"Nope, don't do that either. It's good to know you want us. Don't be ashamed of that fact. " Rob said pulling my hair again. This time more gently than he had a moment ago.

"Though we aren't sleeping with you today so let's get you changed and into comfy clothes for a movie marathon." Jake said releasing his hold on my chin so Rob could guide me to the bedroom with his hand still in my hair.

"You know this is not helping my libido at all right?" I said as he sat me on the bed, releasing his hold to grab me comfy clothes then shoved me and the clothes into the bathroom to shower. I took my time in the bathroom, letting my libido cool off some and relax before rejoining the guys. I was enjoying the day with the, but the introvert in me need to take a second. Once I left, Rob jumped in the bathroom after me and Jake wrapped a blanket around me before taking Rob's place in the bathroom when he came out. I sat scrolling on my phone as the guys grabbed drinks and cuddled me, since they would not let me leave the couch anyway. I tried once and was instantly shoved back down.

"Are either of you going to tell me where you hid my laptop by any chance? I could get some work done while we watch this." I asked scanning the room for my familiar backpack but not seeing it at all.

"Nope, we hid it for this exact reason. You are not doing any work today at all. It is the weekend. Watch the movie." Jake said before putting on some comedy film that we had all inevitably seen at least a thousand times. I got restless from my position and moved so I was leaning against Rob and listened to his heartbeat increase. Right as it calmed down I moved my hand so it rested on his upper thigh and nuzzled further into his chest.

"Angel." Rob said warningly.

"I'm just getting comfortable." I said, hiding my face in his chest with a smirk.

He snorted and went back to watching the movie. I moved my hand again only for him to grab and hold it in his. I then wriggled my feet in Jake's lap, hearing him gasp and clamp down on them.

"You know what happens to naughty little girls that can't keep their hands to themselves?" Rob asked me.

I shook my head, unable to hide the smirk forming on my lips.

"They get the burrito treatment." Rob grabbed my hands and pinned them under the blanket as Jake did the same with my legs. In seconds the two of them had me effectively wrapped up in the blanket, like a burrito. I pouted at Rob only for him to bop me on the nose with his index finger.

"That's what you get. Keep your hands to yourself and watch the movie." We spent the rest of the day curled around each other and I fell asleep with my head on Rob's chest. I woke up slightly when he lifted me to carry me to bed, where I fell back asleep between the two of them.

Chapter 23

Angelina

My alarm went off Monday morning far too soon. Once again I was snuggled into the two of them and it was becoming far too enjoyable for me. I wondered if I was becoming far too used to this and relying on this becoming a new normal. We all rolled out of bed, Rob laying out my clothes and heading into the kitchen to pack my lunch while Jake ushered me into a slightly handsy shower. I got ready for the day and accepted my bags from them. Rob handed me a travel mug of coffee that tasted far too fancy for him to have made it in my kitchen but somehow he had. The three of us walked to my office where they each kissed my forehead and left me to start my day. Thankfully they hadn't come in because I found Sheila waiting for me inside.

"Ready for the weekly meeting?"

"Not even slightly. Why do we have these things again?" I asked while throwing my lunch into the mini fridge and unpacking anything I wasn't going to need in the next hour, which was basically everything except my laptop and coffee.

"I think they just want a way to force us all here at 8 am on a Monday morning. I know for sure I would be snuggled up in my bed with a blanket if I had anything to say about it." Sheila said.

I snorted in laughter. "For sure." I glanced around the office. "Where's Rochelle? Isn't she supposed to be here too? Or is she skipping the morning meetings already?"

Right as I finished the sentence the door flew open and the tornado that was Rochelle spilled into the office.

"I'm here." She said throwing her lunch into the fridge, grabbing her bag, and heading back to the office door. "Now let's go."

Laughing we followed her out the door and down to the world's most pointless meeting. We found our usual seats at the back and set up to do other work while we waiting on the head instructor who was undoubtedly going to be late again. I checked my phone to see a message from Ryan.

Ryan: Good morning beautiful. I can't wait to see your smiling face again.

Me: When?

Ryan: Soon gorgeous, soon.

I blushed and put my phone away right as the instructor came in five minutes late, to begin her setting up of the computer for the next fifteen minutes.

"This week you all will be introducing the students to the scientific method. The experiment is fairly simple but watch carefully so you know how to combat any questions the students may have." The instructor began, then continued by reading the entire lab instructions word for word out of the manual.

Tuning her out I whispered to Sheila "How did they make it into a science program if they have never been introduced to the scientific method before?"

"Beats the hell out of me. How did we all become instructors if we can't read the lab manual?"

I smiled and turned to the litany of emails that accumulated over the weekend. I'm going to have to put my foot down some with the guys and force them to let me work on my stuff at least a little bit over the weekend, otherwise I am going to get behind something fierce. It took me the rest of the lecture to get through the email chains, but I finished clearing them out right as the instructor asked "Any questions?"

I had no idea what the topic was, but I had taught the class last semester so I'm assuming it was the same experiment. My assumption was confirmed when Kaushal asked "This is the same as last year right?"

"Yes, it is the same. As are all the experiments but the last one."

At her answer all of the returning instructors fully checked out, most likely for the rest of the semester. After a couple more questions that were either answered in the lab manual or were not relevant to the entire instructional group, we were dismissed.

"Angelina" The instructor called right as I reached the door to leave.

"Yes"

"Can you stay a moment?"

I turned and smiled at Rochelle and Sheila before walking over to where the instructor was.

"Two of your students were out last week. One of them emailed me this morning and said he would also be missing this week. Please be sure to make sure they are both appropriately caught up."

"I will. I must have missed the email from him saying he would miss this week too, but I will coordinate with him and check in. Thank you."

"I will be sure it gets forwarded to you. That is all. Let me know if you need help." She said dismissing me to leave.

I practically ran from the room before she could find something else for me to do. Telling Rochelle and Sheila about it when I went up to the office before we all settled in to do work. I'll admit, we were far less productive when all three of us were in the office, but I think that had more to do with the fact that we just enjoyed talking to each other when we finally got the opportunity. All too soon it was time for Sheila's class which meant mine was up next. Rochelle was teaching the last class of the day today, as she was mostly a fill-in for the other sections.

"Wish me luck." Sheila said before rising and heading out the door like she was going to her doom.

"Good luck!" We echoed.

I stopped my work and put on a silly YouTube video before eating my lunch. Rob had packed me a roast beef sandwich and a side of salt and vinegar chips. It honestly just melted in my mouth and was incredibly filling. There were also carrot sticks and a brownie, but I decided to save those for an after-class snack. I would need to ask him where this all came from because I know it wasn't my fridge and I hadn't noticed him making anything.

I could not help but enjoy the moment of savoring a delicious lunch and watching a funny video while contemplating what I did to deserve this. I also was struggling with the idea that maybe I was suffocating them. Did they actually want to spend all this time with me? It's not like they had anything to gain. I also had to think about what to do with Ryan, who I enjoyed spending time with, but probably wouldn't want to join the menagerie of men. I shook the thought out of my head and focused on the positives. I needed just to relax and enjoy the moment and not read so heavily into everything. I finished my lunch and packed up my bag to head downstairs. I waved goodbye to Rochelle and headed down to set up my classroom. I once again propped open the door only this time Jake and Rob immediately came through it and picked their seats near the front.

"Well, hello there teach." Jake said with a sexy smirk. "Long time no see."

"Good to see you beautiful. Hope you enjoyed your lunch." Rob said with a smile.

I glared at them both as much as I could while a smile was threatening to break through. "Thank you for the lunch, I truly appreciate it. However, in this classroom, you do not know me. I am your teacher so no flirting or I will stop everything. Got it."

The boys nodded and glanced at each other a little nervously before grabbing the sign-in sheet and writing their names before the next students came in. They then moved their seats to the back so they could make faces at me in peace. I started setting up the computer and greeting the students coming in, when a familiar voice called my name. I looked up directly into a face that the last time I had seen was leaving me in a bar bathroom, the face that belonged to the person making me smile on the other end of the phone, the face that was crushing my heart.

"Angelina?" Ryan said again.

"What are you doing here?" I whispered, conscious of the other nosy students in the room, especially the two in the back.

"I missed class last week and need to know what I can do to make it up to you." He said with a smirk.

"I don't have a Ryan on my roster?" I asked completely confused.

"Ryan is my middle name. My first name is Marcus, but I don't normally go by it. Please continue to call me Ryan."

I was in shock, he played me. He knew I was his teacher. He just wanted to mess with me. I straightened myself, determined to not let this boy get the better of me. "Last week was just syllabus week, the PowerPoint is on the website. If you have any questions ask your classmates. Now class is about to begin so please find a seat."

Externally I looked calm as he went and sat beside Rob and Jake but internally I was losing my shit. They were friends! They were chatting and glancing at me worriedly so I knew they all knew what was happening. It was all one big game to them. The assholes.

I started class and moved robotically through the slides. I let the class do the experiment and stayed far away from the back corner that thankfully had enough sense to not raise their hand for me to come over. I was not in the mood for any of the games the three of them would feel like playing with me today. I successfully avoided them the entire class and had packed everything up, following the last student out into the crowded hallway before heading upstairs to my office. I was determined to not give them a second where I was alone for them to ambush me. I burst through my office door thankfully seeing Sheila and Rochelle inside.

"Are you alright?" Sheila asked.

"I'm fine. My class was just a lot so I wanted to get away from my annoying ass students."

They seemed to accept that response and Sheila started telling me about her day while I let my mind spiral. My phone began lighting up with text messages.

Ryan: Calm down and let us explain.

Rob: Please do not be mad at us before you know what is happening.

Jake: You can't hide from us forever.

Me: Leave me alone. You had your fun, now fuck off.

I turned my phone off and ignored the persistent buzzing. I did not want to read how they hadn't meant to hurt me when they were playing with my feelings. I was just overwhelmed by the entire thing. When Sheila had packed up to leave I stood and offered to walk with her, saying I would take the bus today. The bus stopped further north of my place, but it would throw off the guys because it meant they could not wait along my normal route for me. Sheila and I walked to the bus in amicable silence, with me sensing she was letting me have my thoughts. I saw no signs of the guys on the bus or while I was walking down to my apartment. I even entered a different way to be sure they could not ambush me before I got in my door. The satisfying noise of the door lock clicking behind me meant I was safe to lay on my bed and cry into the blankets that smelled exactly like Rob and Jake.

Chapter 24

Jake

"Where the hell is she?" I growled at Rob and Ryan. It was well passed her normal time of leaving the building and while I wanted to give her space, I refused to let her work herself to the bone due to stress from us.

"Go inside and check her office." Ryan replied.

I walked inside the building and headed up the stairs, my heart dropping when I saw the dark and locked office door.

"Fuck." I exclaimed before heading back downstairs to the other two guys.

"She slipped past us." I practically shouted at them. I was more than pissed at our Angel for not listening to us or answering any of her messages while also somehow making it past all of us. She must've gone home by herself which is just not right.

Rob put his hand on my shoulder to calm me down even though he looked as irritated as me. "Let's go to her place and talk to her there. She won't be able to hide from all of us forever."

We made our way across campus and headed for Ryan's car which was parked on the next street over. We needed to talk to our Angel, how could she think she could hide from us for too long?

Angelina

I was wallowing on my bed when a loud angry knock on my front door jerked me out of my feelings.

"Angelina, open this door now before we disturb your neighbors and come in anyway." Jake's unmistakable voice came through my front door. Apparently, these guys had no intention of taking a hint and leaving me alone today.

"Fuck off." I shouted back.

"Now, Angel." Rob sounded stern.

At that expectant command, I stormed over and unlocked the door, throwing it open to give them a piece of my mind when the three of them shoved it open and forced their way in. The door closing behind them and Ryan reaching over to flick the lock back into place.

"Better. Now let's talk." Ryan said.

"No. Get out and leave me alone. You don't want me. You just wanted to mess with me. Go away. " I shouted at them. Ryan's face turned deadly.

"You think we don't want you? That this is all a game?" His voice was deadly quiet in anger causing me to back up a couple steps.

"I don't chase things I don't want Angel." Jake said, moving forward a few steps until I moved backward and bumped into a wall. The three of them crowded me against the wall, giving me no escape and forcing me to focus on them.

"We want you. Let us show you." Rob said grabbing my chin and tilting it to his for a kiss. I could not help but moan into the kiss as their hands surrounded me. Ryan's hands sunk into my hair and dragged me away from Rob and into him. I sunk into my kiss with him before Jake proceeded to steal my breath. I was overwhelmed by them, and my anger and hurt was slowly fading with their hands on me. The guided me into the bedroom and started to strip my clothes off.

"Seems like we need to remind you exactly who you belong to today sweetheart." Jake said while stroking his cock. I remembered how that cock felt while grinding on it and seeing it made me wetter before remembering I was supposed to be mad. My mood change must have registered on my face because Rob spanked my ass hard before sliding a finger into me. I was lost in a haze of moaning and noises as Ryan twisted my nipples and used them as handles to pull me down so he could line his cock up with my mouth. He started sliding his cock down my throat as Rob slid his into my pussy. Finally, they were fucking me in earnest. I felt my orgasm building and came with a scream around Ryan's cock as Rob's hips stuttered and he pulled out to come across my back. Ryan then flipped me onto my back to come across my chest, Jake then slid home into my pussy and started fucking me hard and fast.

"Cum again for us Angel and then I will cum on you." He said smacking my tits in rapid succession. I could not stop the orgasm from blazing through me and came with a scream that Rob muffled with his mouth. Jake pulled out and jerked his cock twice before coming all over my lower body. The three of us re-laxed, spent on my messy bed. I was too tired to move and tried to shy away from Ryan's hands as he lifted me out of the bed.

"I'm sorry sweetheart, but you need to get cleaned up." He said carrying me to the shower. I was too exhausted to protest and let him clean me up before he returned me to the now clean bed. Ryan snuggled me into him while the other two went to clean up and then settled in behind me. I drifted off to sleep, exhausted from the emotional upheaval and the vigorous fuck-ing they had given me.

Chapter 25

Angelina

The next morning, I woke up squished between two raging hot bodies. My feet were also pinned down by a weight on top of them. I still was exhausted but delightfully sore. I tried to wiggle my way out from the situation I found myself in only for the arms around me to hold tighter. There was no escape.

"Go back to sleep." Mumbled one of the guys.

"I need to get up." I whined. They may not have plans for the day but I did and I needed space from them.

The arms closed back around me and yanked me back down to his chest. "Nope. You get to stay here today."

I was tempted to stay comfortable in the warmth of the bed but the wave of irritation I felt from yesterday returned and I refused to stay in this bed any longer than I needed to.

"Nope. Let me out. I need to get out of here." I wriggled free from the grasping arms and the legs that pinned me down to finally escape the tangle of limbs and blankets. I stood on my bedroom floor and looked at the three ridiculously attractive men that were taking up my entire bed.

"How the hell did we all fit in the bed?" I said mostly to myself incredulously.

Jake lifted his head and smirked at me "Come back in and we can remind you."

At his words Rob moved like he was going to grab me and I scrambled away into the bathroom. Ryan watching me from his position near the end of the bed. I looked at myself in the bath-room mirror, my thoughts racing as I stared into my green eyes.

What the hell was going on? Was this still one big game to them?

I must have been staring at myself for longer than I had realized because a banging on the door jolted me out of my thoughts.

"Angel? You okay in there?" Rob asked at the door.

I walked over and opened the door looking at his worried brown eyes. "I'm okay I promise. It's just..."

"Just what Angel?" Rob asked a little worriedly.

"How does this all work? I mean what is this? Where do we go from here?" I asked. The words rushing out of me in a hurry.

"Let's go into the living room." Rob grabbed my hand and let me into the living room where the other two guys were sitting on the couch, leaving a spot open on the end. He led me to a spot on the end of the couch. Rob then went and grabbed a made cup of coffee that was sitting on the kitchen counter and sat on the chair across from the couch, facing me.

"What is your concern with all this?" Rob asked, looking at me expectantly.

"What is this for you?" I said quietly.

"You are ours." Ryan said definitively from his spot on the couch beside me. Jake nodded definitively.

Rob nodded and added. "We want you. In the bed and out of it. We want you in our lives and we are damned going to keep you if you allow."

The other two moved to argue with him before he silenced them with a glare.

"You get a choice Angel. One chance to say no to us and we leave you alone. We become your students and nothing more. Or you say yes and you are stuck with us forever. One chance."

"Do I get a second to think about it?"

"No, because you know what you want and whether you want us." Rob answered with his same stern expression.

I looked at Rob's stern expression, Jake's pleading eyes, and Ryan's sure gaze with a bit of worry hidden deep in his eyes and I knew what my answer would be.

"I am your teacher, there would be a level of being inappropriate." Jake started to stand at my words, but I put a hand up to stop him. "But. I don't want to let you go. I am yours and I would not change that for anything." Jake slammed into me, knocking me against the back of the couch and hugging me so hard I was not able to breathe.

"We need ground rules though." I said through a choked voice. "Sex is not going to solve every argument, and I reserve the right to tell you that I need space."

Ryan pulled me from Jake's crushing embrace and kissed me incredibly hard, stealing the breath from my lungs. He pulled back and said "And we reserve the right to give you that space while being right next to you."

Rob crushed me into a hug as well, the relief palpable through his body. He must've held onto so much tension, believing there was a chance that I could ever turn these men down. There was no doubt that I wanted them, but I was still worried about what the future would hold for us.

"We still need to talk about where this is going. What does this look like for the future and in class? We can't get caught or I could face repercussions and you all would be failed." I said moving away from Rob.

Jake grabbed me and kissed me again. "It's so hot when you use big words."

I laughingly pushed him away from me again. "Okay but seriously, we need to talk."

"We can remain friendly only during class and during any times you tell us to. We are still going to take you on dates, and we are spending the nights with you." Rob stated.

"Every night?" I interrupted.

Ryan shot me an unimpressed look.

"Don't you all need a break from me?" I asked quietly, the words from my exes ringing in my ears when they claimed I was too much, and they needed a break.

"Nope. No breaks are allowed here. You get tired of hearing me talk, you sit on my face to shut me up." Jake said.

"What if you need to shut me up?" I said with a smirk.

Jake moved so he was standing so close to me I could feel the heat radiating off of him. "If we want you to shut up, we'll either fuck you so hard you can't form words or stuff that pretty mouth with something so that all I can hear is moans."

I gulped and blushed. That comment made a direct beeline to my throbbing core, which needed to get under control right now.

"If you need space from us, tell us and we will give you some time, but we spend every night together. Whether we are in the middle of a fight or not." Rob finished while Ryan continued to hover above me.

I stepped back from Ryan and backed into Jake who was behind me. He wrapped his arms around me, cocooning me in his arms and against his chest.

"And as for respecting you as a teacher, we reserve the right to be subtly hot for teacher in class. We won't be completely public until it is no longer an issue for you, but you will be ours every day in private" Jake emphasized his words with a hard grind against my ass. My core reignited and I could not stop myself from grinding back into him. Rob tugged me from Jake's arms and into his, stopping my movements with a slight smack to my ass.

"Stop that you two. We don't have time for that, and I am not leaving her wanting all day long." Rob said before looking directly down at me. "Now are you fine with all this or do you still need to talk about something?"

I hid my face in his chest and shook my head no. I couldn't meet their eyes with the intensity I was feeling in the room. I would cave and never make it to the meeting in time and based on their words, I doubt they would turn me down.

"Great," Rob said with a firmer smack to my ass. He really seemed to have a fixation for doing that. "Let's finish getting ready and I will walk you to your lab while the other two go to their morning classes."

We reluctantly separated and the four of us went to get ready. I started on my travel mug of coffee from Rob and accepted a kiss from all three of them before we headed out the door. It felt so domestic for the four of us to joke and laugh together on our way to our morning activities. It was surprisingly pleasant, and I almost did not want to say goodbye to Ryan and Jake when they split to head to their statistics class. Rob grabbed my hand, and we walked in comfortable silence to my lab door. Rob leaned down and gave me a quick kiss. "Text us when you are ready to leave. One of us will walk you home. Don't work too late."

After one last panty-melting kiss he left me at the door and headed out. I walked into the lab and got set up for the day, feeling pretty content with the conversation and choosing to accept my crazy reality. I still felt the need to talk to Sheila about it when she came in though, I needed my girl's opinion.

Sheila came into the lab an hour later with her backpack stuffed full and a cup of coffee in hand. Her shirt today was another metal band that I had never heard of but I loved the design.

"This is for you." She handed me a cup of coffee that she produced from somewhere and I was overjoyed.

"Thank you! You are the best." I snapped a quick picture of it and put a heart before posting it on my Instagram story. I could never express how much I appreciated my friend.

"Well, you said you needed to talk to me today so I figured we would both need another coffee for this situation." She sat down in her office chair and faced me. "So tell me what is happening."

I spilled everything about the guys, the dating app, them being my students, the possessiveness, and our conversation this morning. It all just tumbled out of me without me being able to stop it at all. I waited for her judgment when I finished, not being able to look at my friend for fear of what would be on her face.

"You lucky bitch." She said a moment after I finished. I looked up at her in surprise.

"What?"

"You lucky bitch. You have three men that are obsessed with you, and they are willing to wait to go public. You have won the fucking lottery. What's the issue?"

"The issue is they are my students, and I could get fired!"

"Okay the way you say that is like you are the creepy high school teacher when all of you are adults in your late twenties. Also, they are willing to wait on you, in order to keep everything . Besides its just a shitty IA job. It's not like that was your career past graduation anyway, so just deal with it okay. Relax and have some fun here. You deserve it." Sheila said.

"You're right. I need to just chill." I said, relaxing some and just being happy that I get to enjoy this time with my friend.

"I'm glad they make you happy." Then Sheila leaned in with a mischievous expression on her face. "Now tell me what they are like in bed."

At her words the door to the lab slammed open and Ryan stormed in. The door closed behind him, and he slowed his steps looking around the room. I stood up and he moved towards me, being conscious of Sheila in the room.

"She knows. What's wrong?" I asked.

"Where the fuck is he?" Ryan growled, grabbing me and staring directly into my eyes.

"He who?" I asked bewildered.

Ryan just pulled his phone out and showed me my Instagram story. In the background of the coffee post was Sheila's rock band shirt. I just laughed and Ryan let out a warning growl.

"He's sitting over there watching all this go down." I said pointing and laughing at where Sheila was now sitting smugly in her office chair.

"He fell for the unintentional dude thing huh." She said laughing.

"Yep."

"Explain. Now." Ryan said a little clipped. He had started to relax now that he realized I hadn't posted some random guy on my social media.

"Sheila and I both wear a lot of T-shirts. Apparently, the shirts we wear are not very girly and that has resulted in many guys thinking that we are on a date when we post photos with each other in the background. Her band shirts have caused most of it." I said laughing.

"Though my favorite was the guy that called you a slut for posting a photo with a guy in the background, so you sent him a picture of us together and then blocked him." Sheila said laughing.

"So I don't need to remind you of which men you belong to?" Ryan looked down at me smirking.

"I didn't say that." I said leaning up for the kiss from him. He consumed me with the kiss. Making me forget where I was and the fact that we were not alone in the lab.

"And on that note, I am going to take a walk and get back on dating apps. I'll be back in thirty kiddos. Keep it PG." Sheila stood and walked out the door, causing me to laugh into Ryan's chest.

"Thirty minutes is plenty of time." He said, before kissing me more hungrily than before. I started to arch my body into his and his hands sought the top of my jeans.

"Wait, we can't." I said pushing him away slightly, but really wanting to continue.

"We can. Tell me to stop if you are actually uncomfortable." Ryan said pausing for a moment before his hand fully dove into my underwear and quickly found my drenched core. I started panting into his mouth as his fingers found my clit with expert precision. I started grinding down onto his hand, kissing him as fiercely as he did me. My orgasm began to crest and I started whimpering in earnest, realizing I would never be able to stay quiet.

"Let go love. I've got you." Ryan said into my ear.

At his words I could not keep holding back and I let go, my release rushing through me in an instant. Ryan's mouth quickly sealed over mine, silencing my cry and his hand held me up while the other continued rubbing me through my orgasm. As I came down, Ryan removed his mouth from mine and his hand from my panties as I whimpered at the extra sensitivity. He started sucking me from his fingers as I watched him hungrily.

"That's my girl." He said and gave me a quick kiss.

I started to reach for his pants, and he pulled away from me.

"What about you?" I said gesturing to where he was clearly hard in his jeans.

"This was about you, love. I'll get mine this afternoon." He kissed my hair and started moving away from me. "Answer your text messages and I'll see you tonight. I have to get to class." With a smile at me he disappeared into the hall, leaving me exhausted and pleasantly satisfied. I pulled out my phone to see a slew of Instagram notifications and text messages from the boys.

Rob replied to your story: Sweetheart who is that?

Jake replied to your story: Fucking who is that. You don't need strange men giving you coffee.

Ryan: Don't make me come over and scare a college punk.

Text messages to the group "Hot for Teacher".

Ryan: I am coming over. He better be gone when I get there love.

I laughed at the ridiculousness of the three of them.

They were so possessive that it never occurred to them that it could be a friend rather than a guy who wanted me. Also, when did they get added to my phone or social media, much less a group chat between all three of us?

Angel: Calm down guys. It was Sheila.

Rob: Ryan?

Ryan: Can confirm. I still gave her a handy reminder though.

Jake: *pouts*

Angel: Keep it in your pants.

I laughed and put my phone away. They were completely ridiculous, but I was quickly falling for them. I laughed when Sheila returned by banging on the door before opening it a crack and peeking in before coming in. She fanned herself and then sat down while I started laughing. We quickly went back to our work and finished the day with Jake coming to collect me. It felt like all was right in the moment. My research was going well, and the three guys and I seemed to be in a good place. We ate dinner that Rob cooked, and I went to bed between them again. Relaxing into the warmth of their bodies.

Chapter 26

Rob Waking up beside her was something that I could quickly get used to. I just stared at the woman who had fully captured my heart and soul. Jake kicked me in the thigh again, hard enough that I was convinced there would be a significant bruise there in a day or so. We did need to get her a bigger bed or bring her to the house if we were going to keep comfortably sleeping together though. I slipped out of bed with Jake taking my place beside our beautiful girl. Ryan acknowledged me getting up by raising his head and then quickly snuggling back into our girl's back. I went to the kitchen and pulled the stuff to make her coffee out of the previously empty corner cabinet. I don't think she ever noticed where I put it after the first time I made her one and I loved that she trusted me with something so essential to her every morning. The smell of the coffee pulled Angel out of bed, and she joined me in the kitchen with a smile and a reach for the cup of coffee I had made her.

"Sleep well gorgeous?" I asked as she snuggled me and the coffee at the same time. She grunted something that sounded like an affirmative, but I could tell that she was not fully awake yet today.

"Are you staying in your apartment today or are you working from the lab?" I asked the sleepy girl.

"Staying home." She said.

"Okay. I think Jake doesn't have classes today so he might stay and work from here with you. I have to go soon and head to stats class." I said while breathing her in. I could happily start every morning with her in my arms.

"Okay." She said still continuing to snuggle into me.

Jake sleepily came out of the bedroom, and I handed her off to him. He snuggled into the sleepy girl as I finished getting ready and headed out the door with Ryan. If this day was the start of the rest of our lives, I would not be mad at this.

Chapter 27

Angelina

The next couple of days went smoothly as I settled into a routine with the guys. While we were getting ready Friday morning my phone dinged with a text message from Sheila.

Sheila: You coming to the grad social tonight. Or are your hot guys keeping you prisoner for the night?

Oh fuck I had not even thought about mentioning the grad social to the guys again. Considering how they reacted to the last one, this might not end very well. I laughed at the thought.

Me: LOL I'll talk to them about it and let you know.

Sheila: Let me know if you need someone to help you break out.

"What is so funny pretty girl?" Rob asked.

"Sheila was asking me about the graduate student social tonight." I answered.

"Oh?" Rob quirked up his eyebrow. The other two turned towards me with expectant expressions.

"And I plan on going to it." I said, meeting Ryan's intense gaze.

"You do?" Ryan said, moving forward.

"Yes." I gulped.

"So, you want a repeat of what happened last time you went to a bar without us?" Ryan said.

"I seem to remember you all being there." I said smirking at them while a hot flush moved through me at the memory.

"Do we need to refresh your memory again?" Jake said taking a step toward me.

"No" *Well maybe.* I shook my head. "No, but I still need to spend time with the other students. This is how we make connections and vent about our students."

Jake pulled me into him. "But teach, I have something pressing to share with you." He ground his lower half into me in a way that made what he wanted to share all too clear.

I laughed and pushed him away. "I'm going and you all can pick me up after. I promised I will only have one drink and it will be fine."

"Get sloppy drunk or flirt with another man again and we will make last time look tame. You'll feel us for a week." Ryan said. "Got it?"

I just nodded rapidly, and the guys seemed content with that answer.

We finished getting ready for the day and all of us headed out to the campus. It was a beautiful day, and the walk did little to calm my body from their comments. I was so happy just being near them, but the constant presence of the guys was a little exhausting some days. Jake and Ryan split off again while Rob continued his normal trend of walking me to my office.

"Be good this evening all right?" He said, kissing my forehead. He waited for me to nod then he headed out to do whatever it was he did all day.

Chapter 28

J ake

"Why are we letting this douche nozzle flirt with our girl?" I asked. Ryan, Rob, and I were sitting at a back table in the bar where Angel was with her grad friends. I was pretty sure she knew we were here but couldn't see us from her current spot at the table full of grad students. The guy from last time was trying to talk to her again, though she was in a conversation with another one of the girls on the side away from him. I was ready to go give the guy a piece of my mind, but Rob was not letting me leave the table.

"Because our girl is responsible for shooting him down here. We can shoot him later." Ryan said taking a sip of his beer.

"Nope, no shooting anyone in public. We do not need to cause any issues for Angel here." Rob paused and took a drink from his beer. "Besides, Angel will do the right thing. If she doesn't then we can have our fun later."

The guy reached across the table and grabbed Angel's arm. She quickly jerked herself away from him, but I was ready to go over there and kick his ass for daring to touch her. Thankfully her voice carried over to us, stopping me from sprinting across the bar.

"Do not fucking touch me." Angel said, sounding more pissed than I had ever heard her. I got hard from hearing her tone.

"What? I just wanted your attention. You have been ignoring me all night." The dead douche said with a sleezy pout.

"I was talking with Dani and you can talk to someone else. I am not interested in you and I am trying to be nice about it." She looked him up and down and blatantly stared at the beer stain on the front of his shirt. "Besides you are drunk. Go get some water. This is a work event."

Angel walked away from him to the bathroom and a couple of the girls followed her. The douche stood there watching her with a frown, obviously pissed about her words.

"That's my girl." I said very turned on from watching Angel reject another man.

Ryan hit me in the shoulder. "Our girl asshole."

I shrugged still watching the dude and making sure he did not follow her into the bathroom even though I longed to do the same.

"I am so going to reward her when we get her home." I said envisioning taking Angel apart slowly until she had her hands tangled in my hair trying to push me away and tug me closer at the same time. Rob hit me to get me out of my glorious vision.

"First we need to deal with this idiot." He said pointing to the douche who was still glaring at Angel as she returned to the table, pointedly ignoring him. The graduate students started to trickle away, with one of the other guys grabbing the douche and forcing him to head out to the parking lot.

"I'll be back." I said standing to follow the guy into the parking lot. Ryan stood to follow me while Rob made himself comfortable at the table. One of us needed to stay here to be sure that Angel would not come into the parking lot and stop us. This dude needed to learn a lesson. The douche was in the parking lot alone, pacing and staring at his cell phone. He seemed to make himself more and more agitated in the minute it took us to reach him.

"You good dude?" I asked far more casually than I felt.

"Yea, yea fine." He said dismissively waving his hand at the two of us. "This bitch just rejected me again and I need to give her space to get her mind right."

Oh no, he fucking did not call our Angel a bitch.

"Your girl mad at you or something?" Ryan said, stepping slightly in front of me to stop me from decking the asshole right then and there.

"She is not my girl yet, but she will be. You know how they like to play hard to get." The dead man said while smiling at us.

"Is that so?" Ryan said with a smile while moving around so one of us were on either side of the idiot.

"Yea. You just got to get them a little drunk and then they are led around by their pussy. Doesn't matter how smart they are, the nerds fold even easier. Frigid bitches just need a little warming and they are good to go."

"Can I hit him now?" I said looking at Ryan.

"What?" The fucker said before a nod from Ryan sent my fist smashing into the bastard's face. His nose broke under my knuckles in a satisfying crunch. He hit the ground and bounced his stupid head off the pavement so hard he went still.

Ryan raised his eyebrow at me. "Did you kill him?"

I leaned down and slapped the fucker who stirred. Once his eyes registered me he tried to scramble back, slamming into the car behind him.

"Unfortunately, not."

Ryan leaned down and got face to face with the idiot. "If you ever come near Angelina again, what we do to you tonight is going to seem like child's play. If you so much as look at her again, you won't have eyes to see her. Got it."

The douche nodded his head rapidly, seemingly calming down as if it was over.

"Good." Ryan said before taking the dudes head and slamming it into his knee, so he was well and truly knocked out.

I kicked him once for good measure before we left him in the parking lot, bleeding and unconscious. We went back to the table where Rob handed us fresh cold beers to ice our knuckles while we continued watching our girl talk to her friends. As she started looking around for us we made our presence known and gestured to the side lot where our car was parked. We waited for her to walk to the car, before following and meeting her in the parking lot.

Angel glanced at my knuckles and took my hands causing me to hiss in pain. "What the fuck happened?"

I shrugged and kissed her hard to distract her, putting her in the back seat with me forcing the other two idiots to sit in the front and watch.

She moaned deliciously into my mouth as Rob put the car into drive. "Keep your clothes on you two, until we get home."

I pulled away and pouted at the guys while my hand made its way into Angel's pants. She arched her lower half towards my hand while her lips continued to attack mine. Her panties were soaked and my fingers quickly found their way to her heated center, plunging into her and wrenching a moan from her. A short stop at a light forced my fingers deeper into her. Ryan turned around in the passenger seat to watch the show our girl was putting on. Rob met my eyes in the rearview mirror. I kept her squirming right on the edge the entire fifteen-minute drive to her apartment, her moans becoming breathier and needier as time wore on. Once we were back at her place I lifted her out of the backseat while Rob used her keys to open the door, Ryan slammed it closed behind us and I threw Angel on the bed where she landed with a bounce.

Chapter 29

Angelina

My three guys stood at the side of the bed and stared at me hungrily for a moment before pouncing on me and stripping me bare in an instant. There was no gentle caresses or flirting, their actions were firm and claiming. They hardly said anything, and I was moved and positioned as they wished. I had no idea whose hands were whose all I know is quickly all three holes were claimed and filled. We fucked our way through the night and passed out spent and exhausted until morning.

Chapter 30

R ob
The weekend passed in a flurry of fun and relaxation. Simply spending time with my girl and best friends was the precise thing I needed after this week. We teased and played with her some throughout the days, but the majority of the time was spent simply being in each other's presence. On Sunday I was cooking dinner when a pair of beautiful arms slipped around me.

"What are you making over here?" Angel said into my back. She was not that much shorter than me, but enough for her to not be able to see over my shoulder without standing on her tiptoes.

I took one hand and placed it on hers while I kept cooking. "I am making stir fry since it is one of the only things that Jake's picky ass will actually eat."

"Hey." sounded Jake and I felt Angel being pulled away from me as she laughed. I looked over to see Jake pinning her on his lap on the couch, tickling her and making her laugh. Ryan and I met each other's eyes and nodded, knowing it did not get much better than this.

Chapter 31

Angelina

Waking up on Mondays was about ten times harder when you had three warm, handsome men keeping you trapped in it. I shoved Rob and he went off to work his magic in the kitchen, I swear one of these days I am going to have to ask him how he makes my coffees. I escaped Ryan's clutching grasp and went to the bathroom to start getting ready. Jake had my clothes laid out on the bed over top of where Ryan was still lying under the covers. Of all the guys, he was the one who really hated getting up in the mornings. He did not stir until I was fully dressed and ran my fingers over his scalp, his hand coming up to try and catch mine.

I moved away from him and went into the kitchen where Rob handed me a coffee and a bagel. I headed out with Rob while the other two took their time in my apartment getting ready. I still was not sure where they were always getting clothes from, but they always seemed to have a fresh supply and my laundry was always done so I was not going to complain. Rob and I walked in companionable silence, his hand and shoulder brushing mine with the closeness as we walked. I smiled as he dropped me off at my office door.

"See you in class teach." and with a kiss to my forehead he walked down the hallway with a little swagger in his steps.

I shook my head and laughed while opening the door to find Sheila and Rochel there. A glance at Sheila told me she wanted to hear all about my weekend, but Rochel's presence stopped me. The three of us headed down to the weekly meeting a few moments later which was once again unimpressive. This time though I was stopped at the exit by Kendal.

"Your student is coming back this week so be sure to let me know if you have issues getting him up to speed." She said a little haughty.

"Considering the last two weeks are basic stuff and he has been emailing me, I think it will be fine. I appreciate your concern for students though."

"Well, it is my job as the most senior TA teaching this course."

Sheila popped over my shoulder as if she had been waiting for an opening. "That's right, you started teaching this course in your master's program. While Angel was at another university and then teaching a senior-level ID course that was given to an associate professor since no other TA could handle the full class. But yes, we appreciate your experience."

Kendal looked as if we had slapped her around the face and the two of us barely made it back to our office without laughing.

Rochel came in as we were still nearly crying from laughter. "You two left me."

Sheila and I looked at each other and broke out into laughter again.

I got myself under control. "Sorry, sorry. We were being mean to someone else, and I had to prevent a murder."

"Whose?"

"My money was on Kendal's but honestly who the hell knows."

Sheila threw her pen at me as I started laughing and we explained what had happened at the end of the meeting. It was a little mean, but damn did it feel good putting that bitch in her place. She was the most junior PhD student in the department, but she acted the way she did because she also did her master's here. It was insufferable and if she was not constantly mean to us all the time, we wouldn't be so mean back.

The rest of the day passed in normal companionship as we all settled into our work and headed out for other responsibilities. I ate the leftover stir fry that Rob had packed me for lunch and then headed down to teach the class my guys were in.

Ryan

Angel showed up to the classroom fifteen minutes before class started as she always did. We let her open the room before the three of us slipped in behind her unnoticed. She jumped when she turned around and saw me directly behind her.

Her hand went to her chest like a debutant. "You guys scared the absolute shit out of me."

"Sorry love." I said before grabbing her face and kissing her so deeply that she moaned into the kiss, temporarily forgetting where she was. Rob and Ryan moved to block us from the doorway as it opened to admit the next students and Angel rightened herself. I hated letting her go when she looked so positively fuckable, but she would be angrier if anyone else saw her in my arms. The three of us went to our seats in the back of the class to watch our girl. She greeted so many of the students by name, despite it only being the third class. We watched with barely any interest until one smarmy fucker swaggered up to her.

"Hey, I'm sorry to have missed the first two weeks. Is there anything I need to know to catch up?" He said smiling at our girl.

Jake was staring at the fucker as if he could will him to burst into flames with his mind.

She smiled back at him. How dare he get to see her smile! "All the stuff is on the website but honestly none of it really has any bearing on what we are doing this week. If you have any questions you can send me an email."

"I really work better when I can talk to people face to face. When would I be able to talk to you?" He said with a cocky smile that did nothing to hide where his thoughts were going.

"I have office hours on Thursdays. If that time does not work then we can figure out another time. But you really should not have any trouble with the material." She said with another smile.

"Great! I look forward to seeing you again." The cocky fucker said with a smile and sitting down on the opposite side of the room. I was ready to get up and smash his face in but a hand from Rob stopped me from doing so. I looked to see his other hand was restraining Jake and he shook his head at us both. Angel moved in position to begin the class and looked at the three of us quizzically. We just smiled at her with the most seductive smiles we could, causing her to blush before speaking.

"Alright everyone, let's get started so we can get finished as soon as possible." Angel launched into her lecture about genetic expression before we could begin our experiment counting kernels of corn. I wasn't sure what it was supposed to show us, but I took the ear of corn from her when she handed it to me, watching Jake's stealthily grace her thigh hidden from the rest of the class by Rob's body.

"Thank you Angel." I said causing the blush to return to her face. She continued handing the corn to the rest of the class, waiting to give the one to the smarmy idiot last.

"Thank you teach." He said taking it from her in a way that touched her hand. I burned in rage at his audacity. We were going to have to wash him and any other idiot from her body as soon as we could. How it sucked to not be able to claim her in public, in front of all these idiots who wanted to make her theirs. They were not even worthy to be in her presence, much less act like they could touch her. The idiot started chattering away to her, not realizing how his every action and word brought him one step closer to his death.

"Excuse me. Could you please help us with our data sheet? I think we messed it up." Rob said raising the hand that was not holding Jake down to get Angel's attention. I barely held down a chuckle at the annoyed look on the idiots face as Angel eagerly headed over to stand beside Rob.

"What seems to be the issue here boys?" She while standing so that I could see clearly down her shirt as she bent over. While I appreciated the view, Jake was banned from picking out clothes if they were going to provide all these idiots a view of something that was ours.

"Our issue is you talking to a man that is flirting with you, when we can't claim you." Jake said quietly. "If he touches you again, he is going to lose the hand and you are getting a spanking."

Angelina gulped. "You cannot ask me to ignore my students."

"Not ignore them sweetheart, but you do not need to flirt with them or them with you. Just remember who you belong to or we can always remind you." Jake said with a hand moving in a way that was blocked by Rob but got our girl all flustered. "Got it?"

She nodded rapidly and moved away from us, pointedly not looking in the douchebag's direction. As the class ended only the steading hand from Rob kept me from following the idiot into the hallway and making sure he knew never to touch her again, but that would make issues for our girl. Once the classroom had completely emptied I grabbed her and pinned her against the wall with a kiss. Rob and Jake quickly followed me, not giving her a single second to catch her breath in between. We left her panting and gasping against the wall, her pupils blown, and her cheeks flushed.

"We will see you at home gorgeous." I said with a smile, leaving Rob in the classroom to ask her when he was walking her home.

Chapter 32

Angelina

The rest of the week had passed in a blur. Mostly normal until we received an email Thursday evening stating there was a mandatory Friday morning meeting that all graduate students must attend. They even said they would use professors to cover classes if anyone was teaching during the meeting time. I mentioned it to the guys and Rob walked me to the building Friday morning like he had for the past week.

I walked into the meeting where it seemed like the entire group of biology graduate students were gathered. I quickly located Sheila near the back of the room and moved to sit beside her.

I whispered the Sheila. "What is all this about?"

"I have no idea. Apparently a TA got fired suddenly and now we all have to hear about why. It must be a pretty big deal because half the department admins are here and none of them look happy" Sheila replied seemingly just as confused as I was. Nick came into the auditorium looking like someone had hit him with a truck. His nose was obviously broken and his two black eyes were swollen so badly that I was surprised he could see out of them.

"What the hell happened to him?" I asked Sheila.

"Not a clue. It looks bad whatever the hell happened."

I looked at her and laughed a little. "Do you know anything today?"

Sheila shrugged and laughed. "Apparently not."

Nick attempted to keep his head down as he came into the room. When he saw me, he turned and walked in the other direction. He seemed to want to get as far away from me as possible. When he found a seat, he put on a pair of dark sunglasses and shrunk a little in his seat, looking around a little paranoid as if he expected someone to jump out and hit him again.

Weird. Maybe what I said to him at the social last week really affected him.

I made a note to try to talk to Nick later and make sure he was okay and there were no hurt feelings between the two of us. The graduate students slowly stopped trickling in as the auditorium became mostly full. Once everyone had found their seats the head biology professor began the meeting. He was a man of about 60 with white hair and a frame that reminded me of those long-distance runners. He stood at the front looking incredibly uncomfortable with having to speak to all of us today. "Alright students I have brought you all here to discuss the policy regarding intermingling of students and TAs."

Oh fuck.

"I know this is awkward but it is a serious matter. Recently there has been an uptick in comingling which is strictly not allowed. This mingling includes any fraternization with students in your course or your section. Any relationships with students should be declared by the start of the semester. In no circumstances should a relationship begin after the semester begins." He paused and glanced around the room. " I know many of you are the same age as the students you are teaching but that is no excuse for being unprofessional. Any TA caught violating this policy will be removes as an instructor and may face penalties in their program. Please contact me if you have any questions or anything to report."

The professor kept speaking but I could not focus, move, or breath. I did not realize the meeting ended until Sheila grabbed me and led me upstairs. I sat in my office chair, not fully breathing with how fast my mind was racing.

I could lose everything because of them. What if they don't actually like me and this is just one big joke? Are they worth the risk? What if they also get kicked out of the program?

"Angelina, hey are you okay?" Sheila said snapping her fingers in front of my face and forcing me to focus on her. My eyes focused on her even as my mind continued racing.

"Are you okay?"

"What? Yea? I'm fine." I said shakily.

"You don't look fine. Don't stress over this. I know those guys care about you and no matter what you think, the real thing is worth a little bit of stress. That policy is put into place to protect against unfair abuse, you are not doing that." Sheila forced me to look at her. "You hear me. You deserve them. You are not giving them unfair advantages or taking advantage, you are doing nothing wrong."

"I, I, know. It just scared me quite a bit. I just need to go home and relax. " I said, standing to gather my stuff and head home so I could break down in peace.

"Oh, okay. Well call me if you need anything or someone to talk to. I'll check in with you this weekend." Sheila said looking at me worriedly.

I simply nodded and finished shakily packing my things to walk home. I was mentally drained and needed to go home to where I could break down in peace. I walked into the hallway only to be stopped by a person calling my name.

"Angelina. Where are you going?" Rob said catching up to me in the hallway. I hadn't seen him anywhere, so I wasn't sure if he had been waiting for me or if he was just in between classes.

"Home." I mumbled still trying to walk out of the building before I completely lost it.

"Well wait and I'll go with you." He said grabbing my arm.

I yanked myself away from him, not wanting anyone to see us touching, especially after the meeting all the graduate students had sat through.

"What the fuck?" Rob looked hurt and confused at my actions. "Angel are you okay?"

I couldn't answer him without crying and making a scene which is the last thing we all needed right now. I just needed to get away from here and get my mind to focus on anything else before I drew more attention to the two of us.

"I need to go. I'll see you later." I said before rushing away from him faster than he could grab me. My phone continuously vibrated in my pocket, most likely from texts from the guys. I ignored every single one and kept my head on a swivel to avoid them. I just needed to get home alone so I could process and then everything would be fine. I sped walked the entire way and sighed in relief when I realized that I had made it back to my place before any of them. I slumped onto my couch and let my mind run wild and suddenly I knew exactly what I needed to do.

"Open the door Angel." Jake yelled through my front door. I calmly stood up and walked over to the door to open it. Jake, Ryan, and Rob stumbled through the door seemingly surprised by my mood and the fact that I opened the door without any form of fighting. I turned away from them as they entered and went and sat down in the chair, not looking at any of them. The guys stayed a distance away from me, almost as if they were afraid to get too close to me.

"What the fuck happened and why aren't you answering any of our messages?" Ryan asked.

"We need to talk." I said still looking at the floor.

"You are damn right we need to talk. What is going on?" Jake said. He acted as if he wanted to move closer to me, but Rob stopped him with a head shake.

"Do you want to explain to us what is going on sweetheart? Or are you going to leave us standing here and guessing?" Rob said, sounding the calmest of the three.

"We can't keep doing this." I said quietly to the ground.

"What did you just say?" Ryan said in a tone that took no arguments.

I shot my head up and stared at the three of them, determined to make it stick this time. "We. Can't. Keep. Doing. This. I am done."

"You want to explain what is causing the temporary insanity? Cause baby girl there is no done. We are in this for the long haul. You already had your chance to leave, and you said yes so you are ours for life." Ryan said.

Rob looked concerned and Jake looked like I had shot his dog right in front of him. He was a mixture of depressed and pissed off.

"If we stay together you all could get kicked out of the class or the university. I could be fired for being with you. It is not worth the risk right now."

Ryan grabbed my chin and forced me to look at him. "You are worth every possible consequence the world could give me for loving you. I refuse to be without you because of some bullshit rule that does not apply to people who actually give a shit about each other. You are ours and you better not forget it."

"But."

"Say one more word and you won't be able to sit down for a week."

I quickly closed my mouth. They were serious. Jake and Rob were backing up every word Ryan said with their body language, and I was helpless to resist him. How was I supposed to protect them is they would not give me up?

"Whatever you are thinking, fucking stop it." Rob said. "We are not leaving you and you are permanently stuck with us. Let's go to bed."

"Bed?" I asked.

Ryan turned his face up in a grin. "Oh sweetheart, that was a word."

I gulped and tried to back away from Ryan who tutted at my movements and caged me against the wall with his body.

"Tut, tut, sweetheart. I told you what would happen. Now turn and face the wall before I make you face it."

I must have hesitated a moment longer than he wanted me to because the next think I knew my cheek was pressed against the wall and my pants were ripped down. Jake's calloused hands pinned mine to the wall above my head and Ryan started smacking my ass in quick succession. All I could do was cry and take it as he landed smacks on the upper, lower, and middle of my ass. I felt it reddening under his administrations.

"Had enough Angel?" Rob asked leaning in to move my hair away from my tear covered face.

"Good. We will talk about your actions in the morning. Get into bed." Rob said with a slight smack to my ass that made me cry out again.

I followed the guys to bed where they stripped me and put me naked in between the three of them. They put on sweatpants and a shirt and hemmed me in from all sides. They did not comfortingly touch me like they normally did, rather they seemed to pin me down in a way to keep me from escaping. I slept fitfully, with the blanket giving me an uncomfortable reminder of the pain in my rear end.

Jake

I woke before the other three which is unusual. My sleep was restless, and I woke up often to make sure Angel had not slipped away in the night. I got up from my position in the bed and padded my way into the living room to start the coffee pot. I was going to need some form of caffeine and sugar to handle this conversation. She tried to leave us. When she said she was ours. It had been a week and she tried to leave us.

Rob came into the kitchen as I was making my first cup and I nodded hello to him. Lost in my own thoughts.

"Hear her out first. Then we remind her again." He said making his own cup.

"And if she does not want us anymore?" I asked, nervous to hear his answer.

"Then we let her go, but I do not think that is what happened here." Rob said looking far calmer at his words that I was hearing them.

"You better be right."

Chapter 33

Angelina

For the first time in a while, I woke up alone. The bed was empty, and the sheets had gone cold, leaving no trace of the guys' warmth. The memories of what had transpired yesterday flew through my mind and I worried the guys had finally had enough and left me when I heard noises in the kitchen. I grabbed my clothes and threw them on before heading to the bathroom. I was not ready yet to face them. I stared at myself in the mirror and tried to remember that I was not being selfish, I was simply doing what was best for them too. We could not stay together if it meant they would be kicked out of the program. We could wait right? Right? My own thoughts did not sound convincing.

I became less convinced I could do this when I walked into the kitchen and saw the three guys shirtless in my kitchen drinking coffee. The turned and looked at me as I entered, Jake moving his free hand back to grip the counter behind himself.

"Do you want coffee?" Rob asked, his voice as monotone as I had ever heard it.

"Um, yea, thanks. That would be great actually." I felt more awkward around these three than I ever had. Rob handed me the coffee and moved back to his position between Ryan and Jake.

"Do you want to explain to us what the fuck you were thinking yesterday?" Jake spat.

"Can we sit?" I said gesturing to the couch.

Ryan chuckled and moved to sit on the couch with the other two following behind him. "I'm surprised you would want to."

His words reminded me of the pain in my bottom, but I sat on the chair across from them, attempting to conceal my wince. Rob looked at me with concern but did not say anything.

"We sat. So, talk." Jake said sounding harsher than I had ever heard him sound before.

"I think we need to break up. We can't stay together right now." I mumbled at the floor, doing everything in my power to keep the tears from spilling from my eyes.

"We can't or you don't want to?" Jake asked.

"We can't. If we stay together you all can be failed and kicked out of your program, and I could be fired and I don't want any of us to get hurt." I said in a rush, barely keeping my tear from falling.

"And what about you hurting us by trying to end this? Does not that count for anything? Do you not care?" Jake practically shouted at me.

I snapped. "Of course I fucking care. I love you three, but I will not let you face consequences simply because you are with me. We can pause it and wait for a year so that way none of us will be in trouble for any of this."

"Or we can just be discrete. As long as no one sees us doing anything as a couple or group, then we can keep being together in secret and they can do nothing about it." Rob said.

"And what if that is not enough? What if they still find out and we get into trouble?" I asked.

"Then we deal with that if it comes. They would be stupid to fire you and if they try to say anything, we will say we pressured you into it. Deal?" Rob said and the other two nodded.

"Are you okay with that sweetheart?" Rob continued.

I nodded, the tears beginning to leak from my eyes. I quickly returned my gaze to the ground to hide my tears then a hand forced me to look up into Jake's face.

"Now we need to settle something sweetheart." He said with a wicked grin.

I backed away slightly at his words, squishing myself into the chair I was sitting in. "What?"

"You need a reminder that you belong to, and your body is ours completely." Jake said.

At his words, Rob and Ryan stood up and they had me trapped in the chair. At this height my mouth was perfectly aligned with their zippers, and I could not help myself from glancing at them.

"Well?" Ryan said with a quirk of his eyebrow.

I moved to unzip his trousers when he smacked my hand away from him.

"No hands."

I looked at him in confusion until he undid the top button of his pants for me and pointed the zipper tie towards my mouth. I grasped it with my teeth and pulled the zipper down, exposing his black boxers, his cock straining through the fabric. I nuzzled it and started sucking on the tip through the fabric when I could not figure out how to free it. A hand in my hair guided me to Jake's hard cock, freed from his pants and I began sucking on the tip. I teased him with my mouth and moans before he grabbed the back of my head and began slowly fucking my face. I saw Ryan finish removing his pants from the corner of my eye and Rob moved to the side and slowly moved his hands up the front of my shirt.

Jake shoved himself into the back of my throat so that tears formed in my eyes while Ryan stroked himself at the sight. Rob moved his hands to cup my breasts and ran his fingers over my nipples in circles. I moaned around Jake's cock which caused his hips to stutter. He pulled out of my mouth and was replaced by Ryan who started roughly fucking my throat while Rob was pinching my nipples. My hand was slowly moving towards my center before Rob grabbed it and pulled it behind my back. My two hands captured in his one. Rob used his grip on my hands to arch my back and force my chest out. I moaned and Ryan came down my throat with a groan. The second he pulled out Rob pulled me up and bent me over the back of the chair. Without giving me a moment to breath he slammed into me and started fucking me furiously, the moans leaving my mouth silences by Jake's cock.

"You're such a good girl." Jake said while continuing to slam down my throat. "And once we are done you won't be able to talk to us about ending this thing again."

He was right. By the time he finished fucking my throat there was no way I'd be talking for a bit, but I loved it.

I felt Rob's fingers gathering the wetness from my dripping pussy and begin circling it around my ass.

"I think I should fuck you here today. Come in all your holes so there is no doubt who you belong to." I moaned as a yes and they both pulled out of me. Jake laid on the floor and pulled me to straddle him. His dick going deeper as I sat on top. Rob clicked open a bottle of lube and began stretching me with a finger.

"Oh, fuck. I'm so full." I moaned. Ryan reached for me and started kissing me while Rob kept up a steady commentary of encouragement behind me.

"Fuck, gorgeous you're taking two now. One more and I'll slide in. You'll be stuffed by both of us."

"Hurry up. Not moving in her is fucking torture." Jake said from under me. I wiggled and he groaned. "Not fair, so not fucking fair."

I felt Rob moved and his cock at my back entrance. He slowly pushed in and I was overwhelmed by the sensation that I came instantly. Right as I came down from my orgasm Rob and Jake started fucking me, one going in while the other came out so I was always full. The sensation drove me higher as Ryan started playing with my nipples.

"I'm not going to last." groan Rob.

"Fucking come in me. Mark me. Make me yours." I said staring Jake right in the eyes. At my words Rob and Jake slammed into me hard and came together, triggering another orgasm from me. I felt warm ropes of cum streak across my tits from Ryan. We collapsed into a sweaty mess on the floor with me ending up squished between Jake and Rob.

A hand shoved Rob off and out of me to which I hissed in displeasure.

"Sorry love, but you need to get up and wash off." Ryan said while trying to move me off of Jake's chest. His softening cock still lodged inside of me.

"Nooo." I mumbled into Jake, not wanting to move.

"Yes love, you can keep cuddling me once we get you cleaned up and in bed." Jake said into my hair from underneath me. He passed me off to Ryan, both hissing in discomfort when he slid free. Ryan picked me up and carried me into the bathroom where a bath was waiting.

"Come on, relax and get cleaned up and you can go to sleep soon." Ryan said while encouraging me to get into the tub. I slid into the tub and relaxed into the water while Ryan grabbed a washcloth and started cleaning my back and arms. Rob came in for a moment to look at me, kiss my hair and grab a towel and washcloth for him and Jake.

I reached for Ryan. "Get in here."

"No sweetheart, this is just about me taking care of you. Just relax."

Ryan finished cleaning me and helped me out of the tub and into a towel. He dried me off and carried me into the bedroom where Rob was laying on the bed. He had cleaned off in the bathroom sink. Ryan went back to take a shower while Rob cuddled me. Jake followed when he returned, and Rob handed me to Ryan before he went to take a shower. I fell asleep satisfied and happy on Ryan's chest with Rob's arm on my back and my legs tangled with Jake's.

Angelina

We settled into a comfortable routine over the next couple of days. We agreed to keep the relationship lowkey for a while so that I could finish my program and they could finish their classes. Apparently keeping things quiet meant that we were still being touchy in public and areas we were unlikely to be seen, like the hiking trails. I don't think I could ever go hiking without blushing again. We weren't sure where it was going from here, but I was more than happy to be theirs. We fight, we fuck, we care about each other. No idea where this was going or how we would end up, but for now those boys are mine and I'm theirs.

A cknowledgments
      Honestly, this novel took an army, and I am so fortunate to have an amazing one supporting my debut and development of this series. Thank you so much to my roommate, best friend, and all of the incredible people who took the time to proofread this book for me. I could not have done it without all of you! Massive thank you to anyone who is reading this, because I could not have done this without your support.

Thank you!!

www.ingramcontent.com/pod-product-compliance
Lightning Source LLC
Chambersburg PA
CBHW071752150726
47998CB00005B/1903